The Werewolf, The Librarian and I

By: Erin Rambeau

Chapter 1

My name is Aurroara Lee. I am a librarian by day and a werewolf by night. I work at the "River wood's Library." The people I work with are, to say the least special. My manager's name is Jillian Wright, she is a fairy. I mean a real fairy. She has the wand and the dust. Fairies are not as nice as people think. Well she isn't anyway. Dude half the time I think she is PMSing and the other half she is just plain mean. She never lets anyone take any vacations and will interrogate you to death if you call in sick. Everyone except for me. I think she is afraid I will turn into a werewolf and eat her and FYI if she pisses me off enough I will!!!!! The young lady under her is Kasmine Smith, her title is lead Branch Assistant. She is in charge when the manager is not in the building and she creates the schedule. Kasmine is a tree nymph. She is basically a tree, with a face and arms and legs and talks. Being a tree nymph has its down sides, like she is ubber afraid of fire and root rot. It has its up sides as well, such as it makes her really flexible. She is a great ballet dancer. She is limber and can stretch her limbs out beautifully. Then there is Rosa Ackeman. She is the children's specialist and a catix. (This by the way is a cross between her mother a cat and her father phoenix.) She is an orange and red stripped cat with gold wings. She was able to die and rise again, but she wouldn't burn, she would just loose all her fur and be reborn with new fur. She is great with the kids, and patient, quiet and gives them rides. The kids love her. Our teen specialist is Kalila Sweet. She is a humacorn. (Which is part human and part unicorn.) She has beautiful silver flowing hair. The teenage girls love to brush it and teenage guys like to throw hoops and try to make it around her horn.

There are over 17 people who work in this little library and throughout this book I will talk about each one of them. But first let me tell you a little about myself. I am a werewolf. I live in a tiny town in Colorado, called River. It is quiet and not much happens here. You are probably wondering how I became a werewolf. No, my mom is not a dog and my dad who is not human did not mate. No it didn't happen that way. I am a nymphomaniac, in other words I LOVE sex! Well I was having sex with what is now my ex-boyfriend when he got a little too excited and bit my neck. He didn't tear into my throat and start eating my innards. Werewolves actually have self control! It is something they have mastered over the hundreds of years they have been here. They can control it as long as they are in human form, but when they are in werewolf form it is a lot harder to control. Anyway so he bit me on the neck, he tasted my blood. He then bit into his tongue to control the urge to bite me again. He then drew blood from his tongue. As he held himself above me I asked him what was wrong. As he opened his mouth to say "Nothing is wrong I am fine." Little droplets of his blood spilt out of his mouth and into my wound. It only took a week for my blood to fuse with his, and for me to transform for the first time into a werewolf. It hurt like hell. Every bone in my body broke to expand. My two front teeth were extended out into over grown K-9 sized teeth. My nails became claws, razor sharp and deadly. I ran. I ran from the howling, from the claws, from the fur, from the teeth. I ran until I realized I was running from myself. In a matter of minutes I had covered over 100 miles. I remember starting to run back, thinking I have to get home. Then I woke up in my bed, covered in blood. For the first time ever I was afraid I killed someone. I turned on the news. The newscaster was talking about a brutal murder. "Oh god. What have I done? What have I done?" I screamed. I listened hoping it was no one I knew. "The massacre happened late last night. Five are supposedly dead. Only bits and pieces are left of them. The other three hid inside the house and were not harmed."

"Oh my god I killed five people. I am a murderer. Oh shit, oh shit, oh shit!" I fell to the floor and started rocking back and forth. "Help me, I am a murderer." I kept saying. I looked up at the news caster. "We will never know who killed these five today, but we can only hope they have a clucking good time in the afterlife." She said with a laugh.
I sat there dumb founded. "What the hell?" I said.
The news caster at the news station came on. "The police believe the killer of the five chickens to be a dog or coyote. So make sure you keep all your animals safely inside at night. Thank you and good night."
I started crying in relief. I had never felt more relieved than I just did. I hadn't murdered anyone, I just had some chicken.
For the next few days I looked up online everything I could about werewolves. How they lived, where they came from, their transformation schedule so it didn't c- inside with mine, like it would matter. I learned a lot. I learned a lot more two weeks later. Kevin my current ex, is the man who made me into what I am today, came back. He always disappeared for 2 weeks, now I know why.
"Hey baby, whatcha doin?" He asked as he walked through my door.

"Nothing much." I said.
"Cool, want to go have some dinner?" He asked.
"Sure, but I have a quick question to ask before we go." I said.
"Shoot, what do you want to know? And if you are asking where I have been for the last two weeks, I told you I just go to my parents to see them." He answered.
"Why didn't you tell me you were a werewolf?" I guess I caught him off guard because his mouth fell open and the only words he got out were. "Duhh, duhh, duhh!"
"Can I just tell you where I have been for the last two weeks?" He said trying to play it off.
"No!" I said sternly.
"How did you know I was a werewolf? I never showed any signs in front of you! NONE!" He asked.
"Hummm, let me think. Could it be that you bite me while having sex?....No all men do that. Could it be you are very animal like in the bed room?....No that's just human instinct. Could it be ever since you bit me I turned into a werewolf?.....Oh wait, bingo I think we have a winner!" I said sarcastically.
He was dumb founded again.
"Oh god Aurroara….I never….I mean….This was never supposed to….."He stammered out.
"I know and from what I read it is incurable. But I just need to know if there are places to go where I won't kill any people?" I asked.
He starred at me for quite some time.
"Wow, I have changed a lot of people in my time and you are the first to take it so well." He said.
If he only knew that for the first week I sat in my house, with the thought of killing myself. Why you might ask, did I not kill myself. A friend once told me "The world would come to an end if this much sexiness was taken out." As I sat there contemplating death I thought of that quote and how interesting it would be to have the strength of a hundred men and the sight and hearing of a wolf. It took me some talking to, to get me to realize, this wasn't a burden, it was a gift. I can make it and wield it into whatever I want. I am……a werewolf/librarian.
"Hello, earth to Aurroara. You there?" He asked.
"Oh sorry. What can I say I move with the changes in my life. Now what do I do with it?" I asked him.
"Whatever you want! The country is the best place to go, when you change. A lot of animals and few people. And whenever you change back it is usually in the middle of a forest or field and no one sees all the blood on you. So buy a country home and go out there during a full moon!" He said.

"Dude I am a librarian, not a millionaire, I have problems paying next month's rent and I have shit for credit. I can't afford that." I said.
"Then take a change of clothes out to the country, park your car in the trees. When you change you will be in the country. When you change back you can walk to your car, use a wet nap to wipe yourself down and change clothes. Well what's left of your old ones. FYI try to get naked when you change it will save on your clothing bill!" He said.
We talked for hours about changing, sex and getting too attached to people. (This is not a good idea cause most humans can't deal with the idea of dating/mating with a werewolf.)
So now you know how it happened. Interesting to say the least. Me and Kevin still talk, but he moved to Paris for a while. Oh hang on a patron is here to check out some books be right back...............
"Sorry about that."
Anyway I work Tuesday nights 12(noon)-9pm. I work with Kalilia, Peter, Hellzone and Cylia. As you know Kalilia is a humacorn. Peter Pot is an annoying little shit of a poltergeist. He is a clerk, but spends most of his time pushing books on top of little kids, tripping teenagers and pulling the wigs off old folks. Ya we have to apologize a lot for the things he does. Then when the people leave, we have one big laugh. So you could say he is our comic relief. (He is still an ass!!)
Hellzone is the security officer for our library. He is a Hellhound and an interesting breed of hellhound at that. His father was human and his mother was a hellhound. Hellzone got 95% hellhound and 5% human. He looks just like a big black dog that walks on two black hairy human legs. He spends most of his time barking orders to patrons and throwing them out when they disobey him. Cylia is our page (the person who shelves the books). She is a Cyclops. She has very bad depth perception, but is super fast and great at her job. She can shelve books with the best of them.
I spend most of my Tuesday night cleaning up after Peter or listening to people complain that Hellzone kicked them out for no reason, or making sure Cylia doesn't run into the book shelf, knock it over and start a domino effect where it knocks all the book shelves over (every Librarians nightmare). Ya it's happened before. I do help the patrons who are too afraid to ask anyone else for help because they are not human or they see my co-workers as freaks. I sometimes just sit there and think, if they only knew the truth.
I used to be the only full human at the library until the incident. Now, I do believe I fit right in, rather well!!!!

Chapter 2

My work schedule is kind a wonky, if you haven't already noticed. Thursdays I work 9 -1, and then I work Fridays 9-6. It's a great job and I love it. Sometimes I feel like work is home and home is work. I live with 2 roommates. Kerri, who is jobless, goes to school and sleeps on my couch. Kerri is an ex-vampire. She only drinks synthetic blood that has been made in Madrid. It works great for her blood cravings. It also coats the inside of her stomach and it dissolves anything she eats, which is good because the synthetic blood has side effects. These side effects are that it makes her hungry for actual food, such as chips, soda and pretzel. So now I have a 350 lb., 5'3 ex-vampire trying to sleep on my couch. And whoever said vampires don't get moody, are such "liars".
My other roommate's name is Zeban. He is a royal pain in my ass. Zeban is a Furixan. I suppose you are wondering what that is, well I will tell you. The phoenix has many marvelous wonders, burning into ashes and being reborn from them. They also have a wondrous reproductive system (the females do anyway) A single female can have sex with 15 different males and the offspring will have traits from all 15 different males. This is how most new races are formed. Zeban's mother was a phoenix and his father was (he only had two thank god!) was Aries god of war and a human. So basically Zeban has a human body from is human father; gold, red and yellow wings he got from his mother. He has a temper like no other, from his father the God of war. But he was still fun to be around.

Listening to me babbling on, I have to go to work. If Jillian isn't there I'll write some more!!!

Ok now is this something or what. Jillian has meetings all day today and tomorrow. Ubber Yeah! But even cooler I got an email from her saying we have been asked to be a study group for the government. They want to know if chocolate will make librarians happier. We were given a lot of chocolate and asked to eat it, first 5 pieces a day, then 10, then 15, then 20. All the way up to 50 pieces a day. Hell I see it as free chocolate; I'm game. So since today is Thursday I only work 4 hours so I ate one at the beginning of every hour and one right before we left. I must admit they are very good. You know like those ubber expensive chocolates that taste great, but you can never afford. We all have to fill out survey's forms on how our day went. How we felt and if we were happier. Honestly I felt nothing.

So during my chocolate eating fun time, we did have a tiny incident. Working in a library people think "Shhhhh.......You have to be quiet." Which is true with some exceptions, this is one of them.

I was sitting at the front desk when a norms came walking up. (Norm's is our slang word for a normal human. We do have patron's that are like us mixed breeds and some are norm's) Well this norms comes up to me and asked.

"Have you seen my son?"

My thought was "If he is as ugly as you he needs to stay lost!"

But I was polite and asked. "No ma'am what does he look like?"

"Well he is wearing a light blue shirt, baby blue jeans. He is 3 years old, he has black hair.................."
Her sentence was cut short as a boy who looked 3 years old, with black hair and no clothes on ran by.
"And he has a tendency for taking off his clothes..............." She finished before running off after him.
I started laughing as she ran after him whispering "Mark, Mark come back here."
"Seriously!" I thought I have supernatural hearing and I can hardly hear you. I know that kid can't.
I looked in between the shelves and saw Peter emerge from the shelf itself. I started to laugh even harder when the kid started to run faster as if he was going to ram Peter, but ran right through him. He almost ran into the book shelf but made a last minute turn while in Peter's ghostly body. Next Kerinthia Mays tried to stop him. Kerinthia is a Merlady. (It's what you get when you mate a mermaid and a human). Kerinthia is completely human on land, but in water she is completely fish. She reached out to grab the nudist, but he quickly changed direction and started running down the mystery section isle. He was almost to the end when Catherine Cake stepped out in front of our show boating baby nudist. Now Catherine our page for Thursdays, she is a Pegataur. (Half Pegasus, half Minotaur.) Unfortunately for Catherine she got the shit end of the stick. Catherine (or Tear, as we call her) had the body of a Pegasus and the head and face of a Minotaur. When the little shit saw Tear he turned the corner and dropped a deuce. (Or in layman's terms he pooped) He then turned and started running the way he just came from. He was more than happy to go back to his mother.

Our streakier was put into clothes and his mother took him home. (After she cleaned up his little poopie mess he made!) There was no way in hell I was going to touch that. I don't get paid enough to clean up poop! Another crime solved, and another day the patrons of the River-Wood Library can feel safe! LOL!

After I got off work my lovely little roommate Kerri............sorry my LARGER roommate was sitting on the couch doing her school work.
"How was work?" She asked.
"Another day in paradise." I said
I walked over and hung up my coat.
"Oh hey a letter was slipped under the door it has your name on it." Kerri said.
"Really, where is it?" I asked.
She handed me the letter. It was in a plain white envelope, on plain white lined paper. It read:

Hello,

You don't know me, but I have been watching you. You are strong, bold and beautiful. Our paths must cross, for I must meet the one I wish to kiss.

Your Secret Admirer.

"Umm, ok? Did you see who put it under the door?" I asked.
"No, but I can tell you his blood type, it is O+" She said.
"Nice, but not helpful!" I said.

I decided to ignore this letter after all I am a werewolf, one of the strongest creatures out there. So I didn't have to fear anything or anyone, they feared me. How was I to know that my secret admirer was about to knock down every defense I put up to protect myself and become part of my life.

Chapter 3

A few days went by from when I got the letter from who I dubbed "The blood type O+ weirdo stalker!" I was thinking about shorting it, but I couldn't think of anything to shorten it to. I was sitting at the desk at work trying to think of something good to shorten the name to when a Bat came in. This Bat was blue with a pinkish stripe on the tip of his wings. I really didn't think anything of him. I was to engrossed in thinking of stalker names. He lifted his hand and waved at me, that's when I noticed he was wearing boxers. Honestly I would not think that was anything out of the ordinary, except he was ONLY wearing boxers and nothing else. Bats are not the smartest of animals. Great to use for night vision, for spying on your husband to make sure he is not cheating on you, but HORRIBLE to use as a fashion designer. I just let the "man" go on his way. I wanted to go back to my stalker name picking, but something about this "Bat" intrigued me. I just kept watching him. I watched him pick out a DVD from our "Special Selections". Which are the brand new movies that just came out on DVD. We have to keep them up front because patrons have a tendency of stealing them. He chose "Ironman 2" Then he walked to our other DVD's which are all the way in the back and to the right. When he came back he had about 15 different DVD's. He set them on the counter by the self check. I watched him out of the corner of my eye and noticed him read the back of each one, then pick them up and head to the door.
"Sir, sir you have to check them out." I said.
He walked over to me with his 16 DVD's and said to me without blinking an eye, "These are mine. I brought them in with me."
I sat there and did all I could do not to laugh.
"Sir, I was sitting here when you came in. You did not have those, and they have the Library stickers on them. So would you like me to check those out for you?" I asked again.
He smiled at me and gave me an "Oh shit, I have been caught" look. At that very moment I knew he was going to bolt. I just wasn't ready for him to bolt towards the ceiling, and that was exactly where he went. Up!
"Sir, please come down. Honestly we are not going to beat you for trying to steal our DVD's. We will try to get you a library card so you can check them out." I said.
He looked at me "Liar!"

“Honestly I don’t get paid enough for this!” I thought to myself.
Then Tear came walking over.
“I’ll get the little shit down.” She said as she spread her wings and flew up next to him. She grabbed him in a choke hold and brought him back down to the ground with a body slam.
“Dude you totally need to stop watching so much wrestling!” I said.
She gave me a wink and kicked him in the leg.
“Nah this is more fun!” She said.
Our security guard then grabbed him by the throat and dragged him to the back room, where he barked orders at him for about an hour. Explaining our policies and consequences. I just sat up at the front desk thanking god that it wasn’t my job. I waited for Tear to return to the front desk and asked her to reshelve all the DVD’s the Bat had tried to take. With a rear up on her hind legs to show she wasn’t happy she took the DVD’s and walked to the back and turned right. That night when I finally got home, I noticed there was a red rose on my door step. I looked around and smelled the air. (FYI that was one of the great things about being a werewolf my five senses are heightened to new levels of coolness! I could smell things 20 miles away, see things magnetized 10 miles away. Feel things with a new hand. I could feel something once and tell you every fiber in it. I could taste every little spice that was in something I ate. And hear things that were up to 25 miles away. I loved it!) So when I smelled the air this time I smelled a men’s cologne, and an apple and cinnamon candle. (My senses were so good I could smell the wax from the candle.) I stood there and determined from the strength of the smell how long ago the rose had been left. I came to the conclusion it was about an hour ago. I could follow the scent and find were this “Secret Admirer” lived or I could wait and see where this thrill took me. I decided to wait. I wanted the thrill of this hunt to go as far as I could take it. I walked into the house and found Kerri with a whole roasted chicken in her mouth. Considering not long ago I had eaten 5 live chickens I didn’t regurgitate my lunch.
“Ummm, what are you doing?” I asked, as I walked around her.
“Nothing!” She said. Which actually sounded like “Wuhhing” because her mouth was full of chicken.
“Then why is there a whole roasted chicken in your mouth?’ I asked her.

She gave me a "Oh crap I have been caught I better think up a lie quick." Look. Then sighed and I got a "Fine I'll tell you." Look. She slowly took the chicken out of her mouth.

"I didn't reorder my pills on time, so I am craving human blood. This is the closest thing to a dead human." She said.

"Ummm, no, human bodies are more similar to pigs, then chickens. You were human once you should know that!" I said.

"Really?" She asked in surprise.

"Ya, why did you ever think we were more similar to chickens?" I asked.

"Cause you both produce eggs, for fertilization. Humans are just done inside their bodies." She said trying to sound like a school teacher.

"Ummm WOW, you're an idiot!" I said then walked into my bedroom, were of course another issue was sitting on my bed.

"Hello Zeban, what's going on with you?" I asked. Already knowing from the red in his face that he was ubber pissed off.

"Did you chew up my left shoe, you know the good shoes? You know the ones with the leather straps and black buckle?" He demanded to know.

"No, why would I chew up your shoes?" I asked.

"Hello, you're the only dog like animal in this house!" He stated.

I contemplated this. I am a werewolf and it is possible that during my last transformation, I saw his shoes and remembered a time he pissed me off (which is always) and chewed it up out of spite. (Which FYI I would totally do!)

"No, I would never chew up one of your beloved shoes." I said lying out of my very sharp K-9's.

"What about when you go werewolf, would you do it then?" He asked.

"Never, I don't go off chewing up other peoples shoes. I am not a dog you know!" I stated plainly.

He gave me a whatever look.

"Fine, just keep an eye out for any wild animals about that might be after my shoes!" He said, and then marched out of my room.

I licked my teeth and pulled out something that was stuck between them. It had been bothering me for days. I pulled it out; it was a piece of black leather. Opppppps!

I lay in my bed that night and thought of my secret admirer. I wanted to know more about him, but the thrill of the hunt thrilled me more. I laid there and thought of what he might look like. The perfect man, (well my version of the perfect man) Robert Downey Jr. body (like the one in Ironman) and his little free spirit attitude. His nice and secret life of Ironman and Tony Stark, then the brains of Sherlock Holmes. Does a man exist? Does this ubber sexy, smart, sophisticated man of my dreams exist? "NO HE DID NOT!" My secret admirer at the moment was thinking of me as well. His rugid features, and callused hands were no Robert Downey Jr, but his heart was in the right place. He saw this woman he had met only once as a beauty and wanted to know more about her. But the other half of him, his darker half didn't think she was a good idea. He could kill her with one snap of his wrist. But he was so tired of being alone. Every night laying there with no one beside him, night after night. He chose her from about a thousand of women he had been watching. Why this came to light, and why now he wasn't sure. He had seen her before. Yes it was about a year ago. He remembers she was playing pool at the little bar. He saw her, but thought nothing of it. Why now, what had changed. She seemed different somehow. He followed her home one night. He kept to the shadows; she never knew he was there. That was the first night he knew for sure she was the one. The one he wanted. But would she want him back? Would she stay with him, if she ever found out about his dark side?
"Steady, old man, steady. You have to get into the relationship before you fear losing it!" He said to himself.

Chapter 4

You know, I never told anyone this before, but I have always wanted to be a stripper. But the scars I had received last night, has me thinking "NO!" Before I get ahead of myself let me tell you how my night ended up with me getting my butt smelled and the scars that is now preventing me from pursuing my lifelong dream of becoming a stripper. I got off work at 6pm, which was plenty of time. The sun was still up and it gave me time. I can go home change and get ready for transformation tonight. Tonight would be the first full moon of the month, and I was not about to rip up any of my good clothes, like before. Ya a pair of 150.00 boots, down the drain. And as I learn stores do not guarantee money back on werewolf transformation damage.

So I got home and surprisingly enough Kerri was not eating. Of course she was asleep, the only time she doesn't eat. But that's neither here nor there. I just went by her and went into my room. I changed into my ripped and torn old clothes. I then went outside and jogged to the park with the lovely trees down the street. I started jogging and noticed behind me a man was following me. I circled the block 3 times to make sure, and sure enough he was following me or he had a bum leg. I jogged into the park and hid behind one of the trees. The man was going to get one hell of a surprise come sundown. As the sun went down, my body transformed into the werewolf, I was becoming very familiar with. My fur was black with a streak of red on my back. The red streak can only be seen in the moon light. (This was kind of ironic because my hair is brown except in the sun light, then it is red.) So I stood there and sniffed the air. I smelled.....a....another werewolf. I looked around and then out of the corner of my eye, I saw him. He was a gray, rugged wolf. He was about 2 feet taller than me and looked like he could take on the entire San Diego Chargers. He walked over to me and my first thought was to bolt. But as he walked up to me his demeanor was calm. So I stayed. When he was face to face with me he sniffed my face, then my chest, then my feet. Then he walked behind me and sniffed my hinny. This was unacceptable. I turned and in one swift movement I smacked him across the face leaving a large gash in his face from my finger nails. He got angry and jumped up to pounce on me, but I moved the other way and he fell to the ground. He jumped again at me and caught me this time taking me to the ground. We hustled, scratching and clawing at each other. I wrestled free and stood up. Then I ran towards him and at the last moment he reached a hand out and me being the idiot I am, ran right into it. I was knocked out for a second or two, but that was enough time for him to get on top of me. He was about to bite me and prove dominance, when he looked into my eyes and I saw his face change to a look of familiarity. He got off me and took off to the east. Honestly just a note to all werewolves out there, I am not one who wants to play the hinny sniffing games. Oh and to you aliens I don't want to play the anal probing games either!

I would be changing the next night as well. I just hoped that this night would be more boring and less full of idiots, and less full of werewolves like the one I have dubbed "The Hinny Sniffer." And low and be hold it was. I spent the entire night eating out of peoples garbage cans and I am pretty sure I ate someone's flip-flop. And from the phone call I received this morning, they were my mothers. (Now FYI I have not told her I am a werewolf yet.) So when she called I wasn't surprised.

"Hello mother." I said after looking at the caller ID on my cell phone.
"Aurroara we have 2 serious problems." She said.
"Really and what are these problems?" I asked her.
"I have a stalker!" She said.
I started laughing. Apparently she didn't think it was very funny.
"This is not a laughing matter! I left my flip-flops outside last night and someone destroyed them." She said.
"So someone destroyed your shoes, what makes you think someone is stalking you because of it?" I asked her.
"They always start out that way. A stalker steals your shoes and sniffs them while he is away from you." She said.
"But then why destroy them?" I asked a little lost in her logic.
"Duhhh because then when he gets caught by the cops he can say he didn't take them with him, because he honestly didn't. He left pieces of them behind." She said.
I started laughing so hard I thought I might pee myself.
"Fine, good-bye Aurroara!" She said.
"Hang on, you said you had 2 serious problems, what's the other one?" I asked.
"Oh the stalker only destroyed the left shoe!" She said.

"Oh crap!" I said out loud. I like to chew up peoples left shoes. Great now people are going to find out and start calling me lefty. That's just great! I thought to myself.

"What." My mom said.

For a moment there I completely forgot I was on the phone.

"Nothing. Hey when are Dewar and Lywyn going to be at your house? I have something I want to tell everyone." I asked.

"They will be here this weekend for my birthday party. Remember, you didn't forget did you?" She asked accusingly.

"Forget, never!" I said. (Ya I totally forgot!)

"I just didn't know if everyone was coming or not." I lied.

"Yes even your brothers Dakin and Sterbin are coming." She said.

Ok Dakin and Sterben are my brother Dewar's friends. They liked our family so much that they latched themselves on and didn't let go.

"Ok I will see you guys then!" I said.

"Ok I'll see you then. Love you. Bye." She said.

"Love you too, bye!" I said, and then hung up the phone.

Needless to say I owe my mother a pair of flip flops. Apparently I like to chew up shoes, well only the left ones. Well if my only flaw of being a werewolf is chewing up peoples left shoes. Leaving them to forever walk around in circles, I think I can deal with that.

Chapter 5

Ya my day totally started off like shit and just got worse. I awoke to a banging on my door.
"Aurroara, are you in there?" Zeban yelled.
To my amazement I was. (I couldn't remember where I was for a second)
"Yes, what do you want?" I yelled back.
Without waiting for an invite to come in, he stormed in.
"What have you done?" He yelled.
"What are you blathering on about?" I asked.
"My blue flip flops that my mom sent me from Tai land, the left one is missing!" He said.
"And why do you think I stole your left flip flop?" I asked him.
"No, I don't think you stole it. I think you ate it!" He said.
"Ok first of all I don't eat shoes! (Ya I am a total LIAR!). Two I already told you I would never eat YOUR shoes!" I said. (Ya I am totally going to hell for lying!)
"Ok let's look at the facts. One both of my left shoes are missing. Two all that's left of one of them are little blue bits trailing to your bedroom. Three you transformed last night and four you still have little nits of the shoes hanging out of your mouth!" He yelled.
I wiped my mouth and a piece of blue rubber came off. I didn't know what to say.
"Ummmmm.........sorry?" I sort of half assed apologized.
"What, your 'ummmmm......sorry?" He mocked me.
"Yes, I am sorry I ate your shoes. It was an accident!" I said.
"No it wasn't, if it was you wouldn't only eat mine. Kerri leaves every shoe she ever owned out there and you never nibble hers. I leave one pair out and they get eaten. What the hell Aurroara?" He asked.
"I don't know what to tell you. I like to eat your shoes!" I said.
"No you like to destroy my shoes!" He said.
"Look I said I am sorry. What more do you want from me?" I asked.
"A new pair of shoes!" He said.
"Just call your mommy and tell her to send you another pair!" I said.
He got up and walked to the door. Turned back and looked at me.
"Go to hell!" He said. Then walked out.

I felt totally bad. I had been eating his shoes lately, but still I could not control it. And honestly if it was shoes or humans I would choose shoes any time. He just didn't see it that way. He only saw that I was destroying something of his.

Well I decided since I was already awake, that I would get up. Kerri was on the couch eating cereal. Ok now you know those bowls that are used to hand out candy for trick or treaters at Halloween time? The big, large, gigantic plastic bowls. Ya she had her cereal in one of those.

"Good morning!" I said.

I walked by her. She said nothing.

"Good morning!" I said louder, still nothing.

I ran over and jumped on her.

"Goooo….." was all I was able to get out, because when I jumped on top of her, her stomach was like a trampoline and when I hit it, I bounced right back out and into the wall. I didn't remember anything else until I awoke a few hours later with Zeban looking over me.

"Hey you, how are you feeling?" He asked.

I looked up and my vision was a bit off. No wait… my vision wasn't off it was completely out of alignment. My left eye was looking at him and my right eye was looking at a poster on the wall.

"Oh my god!" I screamed.

"What the hell is going on?" I asked with panic in my voice.

"It's alright, it's alright!" He said trying to use his calming voice.

"Like puppies, it is not alright. I can see 2 separate things at the same time!" I yelled.

"Aurroara, calm down jezz." He yelled.

I looked at him.

"Listen, after you decided to 'Hop on Pop." He said using quotation fingers and pointing at Kerri while laughing.

"You were slammed into the wall. Your eye came out of its socket and was dislodged. We had the ambulance guys come down and fix it. They were going to take you to the hospital, but you kicked them when they tried to take you out of the house. So they had a doctor come down here. He was able to put your eye back in. But he can't fix the roaming of it. He said since you have werewolf blood it will heal itself. So just give it time." He said.

"Sorry I ate your shoes!" I said.
"It's ok. I hated them anyway!" He said with a smile.
I smiled back.
He turned around and pulled out a little plastic bag of dog biscuits.
"Hey who wants a treaty? Who wants a treaty?" He said in his cute annoying voice.
I smiled and said. "I do! I do!"
I called in sick to work. It was Thursday and the thought of having to deal with work and multiple people asking why my eye was roaming was not something I wanted to deal with today. After I got up and roamed the house. Turned out I would rather be at work. So I went in. I showed everyone what happened and they asked if I was ok and if I thought I should be at home. I said no, just let me work in the back away from the public and I would be good. They gave me some books to discharge and put in order on the carts. I sat there and did it for about 2 hours when I started to get chocolate cravings. I went up front and grabbed 2 pieces of chocolate candies, because we are still doing that federal study on "Chocolate on Librarians" and I forgot to eat one at the beginning of the first hour. I opened it and ate it. As I chewed I noticed my taste senses becoming aware of each and every flavor. I could taste the rich cocoa beans, the rocky sugar cane, the silky milk and some vegetable oil and something I could only define as grass. Grass? What the? That was odd. I smelled the other one. The smell of grass was there, not very strong very slight, but still there. I went back up front and smelled the rest of the candies. I got the same scent. I was the only one here with a very heightened sense of taste and smell. So no one could smell or taste what I could. I walked into Kathy's office.
"Hey I just ate some of this chocolate and it tastes really funny!" I said.
"What do you mean funny?" She asked.
"Like grass." I said.
She gave me a "You have got to be kidding." Look.
"I am not kidding. You need to have it sent out and tested." I said.
"Uhuh. That's going to happen!" She said sarcastically.
"Fine! Never mind." I said. Then left her office.
I then went looking for Hellzone. I found him sitting in back talking to a patron about running. The young patron, the age of about 5 or 6 was doing everything he could not to pee himself.

"Hellzone, can I talk to you?" I asked.
He looked over at me.
"Sure . Give me a second." He said. He then scolded the boy again and then let him go.
"So what's on your mind?" He asked as he walked over to me.
"I think these chocolates taste funny. Can you have them sent out to be tested?" I asked.
"Sure. I still have friends that work in the police department I can ask to do it." He said.
"Cool, thanks. They just taste really odd and I think there is something wrong with them. I'd rather be safe than sorry." I said.
"I understand. I'll send them out today during my lunch break and hopefully we will hear something back before dinner." He said.
"Ok sounds good." I said.
At one O'clock I went home and both Kerri and Zeban were gone. I sat there contemplating that coolness that was me, when there was a knock on the door. I opened it. There before me stood a man. He was probably about 37-38. Dark brown hair and green eyes, beautiful green eyes.
"Can I help you?" I asked.
"Sorry to bother you ma'am, but this was delivered to my door this afternoon by accident. I believe they are for you!" He said.

In his hand was a glass vase. It was full of roses. They were white and red, arranged so that the white were on the outside and the red on the inside formed a heart.
My entire face lit up and I smiled.
"They are absolutely beautiful!" I said in excitement.
"Yes they are." He said.
I looked up and noticed he was looking at me not the flowers. I smiled.
"Thank you." I said.
He smiled and walked away.
I opened the card that was with the flowers.
'You have stolen my heart, with the scent of your beauty. You excite me and I wish to know you!'

That was it. No 'Hey let's meet!' or 'Hey let's call one another.' No nothing, just those few 'Beautiful' but simple words. It was a game of cat and mouse and unfortunately I was losing. I hate being the mouse.
I plopped down on the couch after setting the rose on the table and stared at them. I loved them.

I went to work the next day only to find 5 police cars out front and police officers everywhere. I walked in and saw Catherine.
"Dude, what's going on?" I asked.
Without looking at me she said. "I'm not sure! But I do know they are looking for Aurroara!"
"Catherine….." I said.
"What!" She said annoyed as she turned and looked at me.
"Oh my god, everyone is looking for you. You need to go find Hellzone, Now!" She said.
So I set out to find Hellzone. I found him up front by the information desk. He pulled me aside.
"Hey we got the results back from the chocolate. That grassy taste you tasted was pot." He said.
"Oh my goodness, seriously?" I asked.
"Yes, apparently the government wasn't testing the effects of chocolate on Librarians; they were testing the effects of pot on Librarians. Seeing if it was a stress releaser. You having the sensitive palette you do, you tasted it. The police are here and they want to know why is it that you above everyone else; why were you able to taste it and no one else was? I haven't told them yet that you are a werewolf, but your sensitive palette saved us, Aurroara. Thank you." He said.
"It was nothing. Just another day's work for the libraries police dog!" I said.
He laughed, considering he was the libraries police dog.
My day after that got better, until I remembered I had to go to my mom's tomorrow for her birthday party. Ya I was totally dreading that!

Saturday morning I awoke to a beautiful sunny day. The sky was blue, the sun was shining, the birds were chirping. I was happy. Then I remembered today was the day I tell my family about my lovely curse. I sooo did not want to. But it had to be done. I dragged myself out of my bed and plopped myself into the bath tub, and turned the water on. This was a stupid idea because with our water you have to let it heat up or you get cold water. I ran out of my bathroom screaming my head off. You know if I heard a neighbor, roommate or friend screaming I would be like "Are you ok? What's wrong?" But my two roommates did absolutely NOTHING. I was ubber annoyed.

I went back into the bathroom and checked the water, it was hot. I took a nice hot bath and after almost drowning myself by accident because I didn't turn the water off and the tub filled up to full. I got out and dried off. I put on my sexiest clothes, because I like to look hot when I am telling everyone I am a werewolf. Then I put in my eyes (my contacts) and put on some make up. I took a couple of steps back from my stand up mirror and all I can say is "Damn, I look good!"

I walked out to my car and saw the guy who had brought me my flowers from the day before. I waved at him. He starred at me, and then walked back into his house.

"Ok, so the guy is either A. Creepy, B. Insane, C. Gay, Because honey I look good. I'd jump my own bones if I could." I said laughing.

I drove out to my mom's. As I exited the car I saw Dakin, Sterben, Syria, Nama, and my mom and dad.

I was a little off ended on telling them the truth about me being a werewolf because I grew up in a normal household, and now... now I don't know. This would change everything. Would they fear me because I could kill them if I got mad? Or would they disown me for the same reason. One knows ones family and loves them, but people have a tendency to surprise you whether they are family or not. So I walked over and hugged my mother.

"Happy Birthday!" I said.

She smiled at me.

"Thank you!" She said.

I sat down next to one of my most bestest friends in the entire world, Syria.

She smiled.

"It's good to finally see you again." She said.

Me and Syria hadn't seen each other since I had gotten the curse. In fact me and my family had hardly been around each other since then. I was afraid I would hurt them. So I stayed away. Mind you it had only been 4 months, but still. They didn't understand because I never told them. But that was about to change.

Syria was a Night Naginis. Her mother was a Naginia (which is half human, half snake. They resemble a human from the waist up and a snake from the waist down.

They are very colorful.) Syria was a light shade of Aquamarine from the tip of her tail, as it went up the color darkened. When it reached the top it turned a dark blue. Her father was a Night Elf. (They are warriors, stocky, big ears) Syria got her father's hair, his bright blue eyes and his smooth skin. How her father and mother mated is beyond our imagination and we don't ask.
"Thanks, it's nice to see you too, babe!" I said. Unfortunately I call everyone babe, it is a habit I picked up from a movie.
"So we are all dying to hear your news. What is it?" My mother asked.
"Oh," I said. I thought I would have more time to prepare. You know sit there and listen to everyone talk and read their mood. Then figure out from there how to say it.
"Ummmm..... I really don't know how to say this...."I said stammering over my words.
"Well just say it then!" Dakin shouted out.
Dakin was an interesting person; he was what is known as a Zragon. Which is part dragon, part Zombie. His mother a Chinese dragon and his father a zombie. When he transformed he looked like a regular dragon would like. When human, since he got his father's zombie gene and his mothers he looked human with a gray stripe of dragon scales going up each arm. His hair was fire red, and his eyes were pure silver, but other than that human. Being a Zragon Dakin had many wonderful abilities. Such as breathing fire when angry, flying and interesting enough the thing he got from his father the zombie was being a vegetarian. Brains are a veggie, hummm who new! But Dakin also had another ability he got from his grandfather. The ability skips a generation so Dakin got it, it was the ability to shape shift. Now all be it he could only shape shift from a dragon and into a human, but that was good enough for him. It just meant that he could sit inside a restaurant and eat instead of in the parking lot and watching through the door.
I closed my eyes and took a deep breath.
"I'm a werewolf!" I blurted out.
I heard nothing. I opened my eyes and everyone was staring at me as if I just said a joke. They all started laughing.
"Uhuh sure!" Dakin said, "And I'm Attila the hun!"
"Ya, and I'm the Reaper's son!" Sterben said.
Sterben, ok, how to describe Sterben. Ummmm he was special. He had the same mother as Dakin, the dragon, but a different father. His father was the Grim reaper.

You know how people say if you put two angry people together you get an angrier person, wrong. Sterben was very special; he was calm, funny and had a lot of personality. He loved acting stupid, but was very intelligent. He just never used his smarts. He got whatever he wanted from his father. Sterben was the only son the Grim reaper ever had. You see if the Grim reaper touches you, you die. But Sterben's mother was a dragon and had a very tough outer coating that protected her. The reaper did whatever Sterben asked. So Sterben had no reason to get a job, to do anything really. It was kind of funny. But his mother made him. Sterben looked normal except for his skin was transparent and you could see his bones. It was cool you could feel his skin just not see it. That and when he was bored he created fire in his hands, but other than that he was normal.

Dakin stopped laughing, "Dude, that's not funny you ARE the reaper's son!" He said.

"Oh ya!" Sterben said laughing again.

"Oh but seriously Aurroara, what's the news." My mother said.

My mother was human, with a touch of gnome, so she always knew when you were lying. My father was human as well, with a touch of giant. Which probably why I came out half in between short and tall!

"That's it, seriously! I am a werewolf!" I said.

"I believe you Aurroara!" Nama said.

"I know how it feels to have everyone you know not believe you about something." Nama said.

"Oh please, Nama! What has anyone ever not believed you about?" Dakin said.

"My pixie dust! I can create Pixie Dust!" Nama said.

Nama was a Pobbit. Her mother a Pixie and her father was a hobbit. She was a bout 4'5, long blonde hair, bright blue eyes and two birth marks of wings on her back.

"Ok then show me the dust, Pobbit!" Dakin demanded.

Nama looked at her hands.

"This is not about me it's about Aurroara and the fact that she thinks she is a werewolf!" Nama pointed at me then sat down.

They all looked from Nama to me, and started to laugh.

"Oh ya, Aurroara the werewolf, owww I'm scared. Don't eat me!" Sterben said sarcastically.

"Really are you going to walk over here, stretch out your claws and scratch my face all up?" My brother Dewar asked.
My brother coming from a normal home was at one point in his life a normal human. That was until the accident. He was in a car accident a few years back. It killed him. Sterben didn't want to lose his friend, so he asked his father what to do. The reaper told him the secret of life, Vampire blood. The blood would revive him. It did and gave him immortality, but it also gave him really bad gas when he ate any meats raw!
I walked over to him, opened my hand as if I was going to slap him, but extended my claws (one of the very few tricks I learned to do as a human) and swiped it 2 inches in front of his face.
"I could have scratched your face off, but I didn't!" I said.
They all looked at me. I was expecting them all to get up and run to their vehicles and leave, but they did something unexpected. They started questioning me about being a werewolf. They wanted to know everything.
"Does it hurt when you transform?" Dakin asked.
"Can you only extend your claws when human, or can you do other cool things?" Dewar asked.
"Do you become male when you're a werewolf?" Sterben asked.
Everyone starred at him.
"What?" Dakin asked him.
"Dude it is totally possible that she is a transvestite werewolf. It happens!" Sterben stated firmly.
"When does it happen?" Dakin asked.
"In books!" Sterben replied.
"What books?" Dakin wanted to know.
"The one I am writing!" Sterben said.
"Ok, you're an idiot! Anyway so how did this happen?" Dakin asked me.
I told them the story about my ex and the 'Love bite'! They were all very fascinated. Then I told my mother something she totally did NOT want to hear.
"Ummm, Ya I'm the one who ate your left flip flop. You don't have a stalker mom." I said.
She looked at me horrified! I seriously expected her to yell at me for eating her shoe.

“Aurroara, that is just plain rude! I raised you better then that!” my mother scolded me.
“I know and I’m sorry!” I said.
“You should be. Of course I have a stalker. How rude of you to say I don’t!” She said.
At the moment I can honestly say I had the “Dumb Look!” Anyone who has ever had the “Dumb Look!” knows exactly what I am talking about, anyone who hasn’t….. well you don’t hang out with the people I hang out with!
The rest of the afternoon went off without a hitch. I felt like an entire weight had been lifted off my shoulders that afternoon. It was the best birthday ever and it wasn’t even mine!

Chapter 6

So now my secret was out, to my family anyway. The library already new for a while, but I still felt a million times better. I drove into my space in front of my building. I noticed that the street light that hung over my space was flickering. It had been doing that for about a month; it would flicker then go out and about 10 minutes later come back on. I got out of my car and smelled a strange smell. It was human, a male. I looked to my left and walked over to a man laying on the ground. My first thought was "I hit him!"
"Oh my goodness, are you ok?" I asked.
He opened his eyes a little and looked around. As if he didn't know where he was. He looked at me and smiled. Then he grabbed me and knocked me down to the ground. I was so surprised when my face ended up on the ground, that I didn't even notice him ripping off my shirt.
"Get off me!" I yelled.
He punched me in the stomach. Bad mistake!
I pushed up off the ground with my arms, as I did he rolled off my back and onto the ground. I stood up. He got up.
"Well someone has a bit of strength." He said.
He reached out and punched me in the face and tried to tackle me to the ground. I grabbed him by the shirt and lifted him off the ground. I was so angry and pissed off. As I had him hanging 2 feet off the ground I transformed right in front of him. The man screamed and wriggled in my claws. The look on his face was of sheer terror. I was about to tear him to shreds. When I noticed a movement out of the corner of my eye. I looked over and saw my neighbor. The one who had brought me the flowers the other day. He looked at me with a look of uncertainty and unknowing. He turned and ran into his apartment. I looked into the eyes of the man who tried to rape me. I laughed a deep laugh and started running with him in my clutches. I drug him on the ground as I went and when I came to the front of the police station I noticed he was unconscious. I pushed through the door transforming as I did. I walked up to the front desk. My clothes in tatters and I looked like shit. The lady behind the desk looked at me horrified.
"Oh my god are you ok?" She asked me.
"No this man just tried to rape me!" I said.
She looked at me, all raggedy, and then she looked at the unconscious man.
"Ummm, seriously?" She said.
"Yes, but he didn't know he was messing with a werewolf-ess!" I said self assured.
"Oh that explains it." She said.

She came out from behind the desk. That was when I noticed, she was half fawn. She had the torso of a human, but the lower half of a deer. She walked over to the unconscious man and kicked him.
"Yep he is unconscious alright. What did you do to him?" She asked.
"Nothing, just accidently dropped him in a couple of pot holes, he may have hit the pavement at points, but what can I say he was heavy!" I said.
The woman smiled. She took my statement. Her name was Elizabeth. I found it strange that a unique woman would have a normal name. But I guess it really didn't matter. After I gave my statement and information, I then went home. I walked not fearing a single thing. I had just defended myself and won. I stopped in the middle of the sidewalk and started doing baby cabbage patch circle dances.
"I rock, I rock. You don't, you don't. Uhuh. I rock! Oh ya!"
This was taken on by on lookers that I was crazy. (And FYI I think I am!) I was starting to love my life as a werewolf-ess. Ya I started calling myself a werewolf-ess because I totally think werewolf is intended for males. I walked up to my front door, when for some strange reason I had the notion that someone was watching me. I looked around. I saw my neighbor guy watching me from his window.
"Oh god, he must be scared shitless of me!" I thought.
I walked over and knocked on his door. No answer.
"Hello!" I yelled.
Nothing.
"Ummm, look what happened tonight. Total miss understanding. That guy was trying to rape me. And me transforming into a werewolf....well ya it probably scared you, but it's cool. I won't try and hunt you down unless you come after me with a pitch fork and lighted torches." I said.
"Crap I am starting to babble." I thought.
"Look if you ever want to talk, I am more than happy to do it." I said.
I waited and heard nothing. I walked away. I could feel his eyes on my back as I did. I opened my door and went inside. I walked into a house full of roses, roses of every color. The smell in my house was as powerful as if I just walked into a meadow of roses. I plowed my way through the living room and into my room. Where in the center sat a red glass vase. In it a single white rose. There was a note attached to it.

Your raw power is only, shadowed by your awesome beauty. I saw what you did to the man in the parking lot. You have the strength of Hercules, the beauty of Aphrodite and the fur coat of a minx. I do not fear you as an animal, but I do fear you as a woman. I hope you like my gift.

Your Secret Admirer

I smiled and took in the smell of the roses. So this man doesn't fear me when I am a werewolf-ess, but he fears me being a woman, and so he should. As a woman I am strong and smart. It started to make me wonder who this man was. He had seen me, but I had not seen him. I had not even smelled him, but of course I was too busy getting ready to beat the shit out of an idiot. This thrilled me. My life had just become more exciting! This man, this mystery person wanted me for who I was. He accepted me for everything I was and what I did.
"I think I am in love!" I said to myself.
Then my little voice that always has to rain on my parade started talking.
"No it's not a good idea to fall for a complete stranger. He could be a homicidal maniac." My little voice said.
"But he likes me and accepts me!" I said back.
"Seriously, most crazies pray on the weak!" My voice said.
"But I am not weak!" I said.
"True, but he will tell you anything to get you, then BAM! Your dead and chopped up in his freezer!" My voice said.
"Ok first of all I am the most feared animal of all time. Secondly find one man who has the strength of me and can take me down. Thirdly I am happy shut the hell up!" I said.
The voice went quite. I usually have arguments with my inner voice. It helps me understand and work things out. They say people who talk to themselves are crazy; I say they are the smartest people ever.

On Tuesday I drove my car to work and went inside to see a giant cake on the table. On it, it said "Thank you Aurroara." I smiled.
"You deserve that." Jillian said.
"Thanks, but I didn't do much. I just sniffed out the truth." I said laughing.
I cut the cake and took a piece. It was great. Butter frosting on butter cake. I loved it. For lunch Jillian bought everyone pizza and soda. I assumed she was trying to get everyone from suing the library for giving them pot. (And FYI I wasn't far from the truth). She asked us to sign waivers saying we wouldn't sue the library, since they were not aware of the pot either. We all felt it was not their fault and signed, with the condition that the library buys us lunch for the rest of the week. The day started off smoothly, until school got out. Then the fun began. I was sitting at the desk as normal, when I heard a noise from the Far East corner of the building. I stood up and looked in that direction. No other noises were heard. I decided to send Hellzone our security guard to check out the noise. I looked around the corner to where his desk was and saw him sitting there.
"Hellzone could you go and check out a strange noise on the southeast corner of the building?" I asked him.

"Sure!" He said.
He got up and walked slowly to the back of the building. The help desk which was where I was is located on the North West part of the building. So any noise that was heard from that part had to be something big falling. Hellzone came back with 2 young men, one in each hand.
"Keep an eye on these two while I call the police and their parents." He said.
"Ummm, ok." I said with uncertainty.
The two young men stood there with an expression of "Scared shitless" on their faces. I assumed at some point they were going to run. I didn't give them too much for brains cause you could see they were part dinosaur and part caveman. (Sadly yes, dino's and cavemen mated! Hey even cavemen need love!)
So I sat there and half watched the dino boys. They didn't move an inch. Hellzone came back out. He walked over to the boys.
"I called the police and your parents." He said.
About 10 minutes later in walked a T-Rex looking man and a caveman looking man, at this point I had no idea who the mother was.
"Sir, Ma'am the mess is back here." Hellzone said.
Me being the nosey person I am, I followed them back. I walked to the south east corner and there were books everywhere. One of the shelves had been knocked over and the books were lying on the floor.
"What happened?" I asked exasperated.
"The boys were playing lets club the young girl. Only the girl didn't want to play. So they ran around like a couple of 'sorry for the expression' cavemen and tried to club her. Only they didn't expect her to be half Anubian. She is one of the daughters of Anubis. So she punched them into the book shelf and knocked it over on to them." Hellzone said.
I smiled.
"God I loved Egyptians. They always knew how to take care of things." I thought.
The police showed up and took the statements and asked questions. The boys were written up and put into a class called "We are not apes, we are human." The class motto was "Less clubbing, more bars!" I think it was supposed to be funny! I went back to the desk thinking "There was my little adventure for the day!" Little did I know, I was completely and utterly wrong!
At 5pm I went to lunch. I decided that since I had no money I would go home for lunch. There I found some bologna, cheese and bread. I made a sandwich and went to my room to eat. I sat in my room and put in the movie "Julie and Julia." This was becoming my favorite movie, and I was reading the book "My life in France" By Julia Child. So far it was great. I sat in my chair and watched my movie. My lunch was quite and serene. After lunch I went back to work feeling quite happy. But my happiness was short lived. I walked up to the desk and sat in the chair. I sat

there for about 10 minutes when my neighbor walked in. He walked up to the desk looked at me, and then walked over the other person at the desk. I looked at him.
"Hi, you're my neighbor right?" I ask him.
He looked at me and gave me a weak smile. He talked to the other librarian and then walked away. Things kind of went downhill from there. I sat there when a child about 7 came into the library.
"Hi, can I help you?" I asked.
"No!" He said.
"Are you here alone or are you here with a parent or guardian?" I asked. (Our policy is that anyone 12 and under must be accompanied by an adult.)
He thought for a moment.
"My mom is right behind me." He said.
"Ok!" I said. There was really no reason to call him a liar. I looked at the clock; it was 6:17pm.
"Only 2 hours and 45 minutes and I'm off!" I thought.
I sat there and finished my emails and helping patrons, and for the most part IM'ing my friends. At 8:45 I walked around to let everyone know we are closing in 15 minutes and they needed to call for rides, check out their stuff and so on. The little boy was on the kids computers.
"Do you have a ride home?" I asked.
"Ya, my mom is here!" He said.
"Ok!" I said and walked away.
At 8:55pm I walked around and turned everything off, including the kid's computers. The little boy was still there.
"We are closing in 5 minutes, where is your mom?" I asked.
"She is around here somewhere!" The little boy said.
"I don't think she is, you are the only patron here!" I said.
The boy looked at me and said
"That's ok I'll just walk home!" He said.
"Ummm it is really dark outside. Why don't you call your mom and see if she can come get you?" I asked.
"She told me not to bother her, while she was shopping." The little boy said.
"So she is not here with you!" I said.
The little boy broke into tears.
"No, she dropped me off here and went shopping! She doesn't want me with her while she is shopping!" The boy sobbed.
"Ok well give her a call!" I said.
The boy used our phone and called his mom.
"She said she is on her way!" The boy said.

At 9:15pm we were still there waiting for his mother. Jillian had told everyone to go home. But I said I would wait with her. At 9:30pm the little boy called his mother again, she told him she was still shopping and she would get him when she was done.
Jillian took the phone "Ma'am at 9:45pm we are going to call the police if you are not here and have them take control of this unattended child. Do you understand?" She asked.
"You can't do that!" The woman yelled.
"Yes, I can!" Jillian said and hung up the phone.
At 9:50pm we called the police and reported an unattended child. Least to say I got an hour of over time. I guess I can thank the little boy and his stupid mother for that. The mother ended up picking up her son at 11pm from the police station. The police told her that child services were called and that she would be receiving a visit from them soon.

Chapter 7

After work on Tuesday night, I went home and crawled into bed. I was so tired that I fell asleep and didn't even know it. In the morning I awoke to an odd sensation. There was something licking my nose. I opened my eyes and found a cat. I was at first a little taken back by this cat. Then I actually opened my eyes completely and saw that my first recollection was correct, it was in fact a cat. I sat up and starred at this cat. It was gray and black stripped tabby cat. He was so cute. I could kiss him all up. Around his neck was a note. I opened it.

This animal is for you. He is untamed, sleek, and beautiful just like you. His name is Ramses. Named after one of the many powerful pharaohs' of Egypt. I thought it suited him, a pharaoh to live with a goddess. And yes that is what you are, an Egyptian goddess. My Egyptian Goddess Ma'at. She was the goddess of the Ancient Egyptian concept of truth, balance order, law, morality and justice. Ma'at was also personified as a goddess regulates the starts, seasons and the actions of both mortals and deities, who set the order of the universe from chaos at the moment of creation. You do that for me. You are order in my chaos.

Your secret Admirer

"Ummm wow!" This guy really thinks highly of me! I so can't wait to meet him." I thought. But once again no place to meet, no times…nothing. I was a little disheartened. I really, really wanted to meet this guy.

For the next 3 weeks I heard nothing from my secret admirer. I was feeling like he had lost interest. And to make matters worse tonight was a full moon. I put on my normal expandable clothes and headed for the park as usual. When the moon came up I changed and it felt great to be able to stretch. I started to run taking full advantage of my speed. I then noticed the silver werewolf from a few weeks ago, the one I had tangled with, and come along side me. He looked at me and winked. We ran together both trying to out run one another. We ran into a meadow clearing where he jumped up over me, grabbing me by the waist and twisted me over then on to the ground. We tangled and fought for a few minutes, but eventually he won.

He was bigger and stronger than me. I was new to this and I didn't know much about the strength of my powers at this point. As he loomed over me, his giant silver eyes looking deep into mine, I didn't fear him. I was curious. He then opened his mouth and with his giant tongue he licked me on the side of my face. I smiled my wolfy smile. He licked me again. He then got up off me and lay next to me on the ground. I laid there and looked at the stars. Then rolled over and held him to the ground. He could have easily pushed me off and retackled me down to the ground, but he didn't. I licked him on the face. I could tell he liked it. I went to get up, when he grabbed me with his massive paws and pulled me back down on top of him. I looked into his eyes and saw myself. I laid my head on his chest and listened to his heart beat. We just laid there. No one else to answer to, no one to come between us, no one to tell us no. There was just us. I loved it, and fell in love with it. As I laid there I fell asleep to the sound of his heart and awoke alone. Using the shadows I walked back to the house and put on some clothes. I then laid in my bed and thought of the werewolf I had once dubbed the "Hinney Sniffer." I had changed his name to "My secret Lover." I didn't want to tell anyone about him. He and I shared something no one else had, we were werewolf lovers. You know honestly I am sure there are others out there, but I like to think we are special. So plthhhhhhhhhhhhhhhhhhhhhh on them. That was me giving them raspberries. LOL.

I decided I needed to stop lying there thinking about my secret lover and get up. I walked into the living room were Kerri was sleeping. There was a knock at the door and Kerri woke up with a fright and jumped up, whoppers (those little chocolate covered candies) went everywhere. I smiled, laughed and walked to the door. I opened it and to my surprise there as my neighbor. He was cleaned up and he looked hot! His hair was combed and pulled back, instead of his usual wild hair due. He was clean and looked great. I almost didn't recognize him.
"Hello,......" I sputtered out.
"Hi, hey this was left on my door step, I think it is yours." He said handing me a red box of chocolates.
I smiled.
"Thank you." I said.
"Hey about what happened a few weeks back...." I started.
"Don't even worry about it, that man got what he deserved. I was going to help you until I saw you could handle yourself. I would have come to the door when you knocked but I had to answer a very important phone call." He said.

"Oh it's cool. I am glad to hear that, I mean it, I mean.....Ya, your hot.....Oh shit did I just say that out loud" I asked.
He smiled at me.
"No I didn't hear anything. Thanks by the way, you're not bad yourself!" He said, then smiled and walked away.
I stood there with another "Dumb Look" on my face.
I looked at the box of chocolates and taped to the cover was a beautiful red card. It simply read:

Roses are red, violets are blue. I had a great time running with you. I'll see you tonight.

Silver back.

I smiled. It was from the werewolf last night.
"Oh my god, Oh my god!" I smiled at myself. I took the chocolates and handed them to Kerri, who was now wide awake.
"You don't want them?" She asked.
"After the chocolate incident at work, no. I think I am ALL chocolated out!" I said. It was a wonderful gift, and I loved the card, but not as much as the thought of seeing my "Silver back" again. Great I thought to myself. I have to change his name AGAIN! I can just see me trying to explain this to our kids. Children gather around and let me tell you how I met your dad and the 3 different names I called him. I can just see them now rolling their eyes at me and them begging to be let out of the room.

Throughout the day I started singing. Kerri and Zeban couldn't understand what on earth was going on with me. They thought I was going insane, even crazy. Then Kerri looked at me and suddenly out of nowhere figured it out. (Which is a special feat. For her because I think being a vampire has turned her brain to mush).
"Holy Shit, she's in love!" She just blurted out.
I ignored her. It was NONE of their business anyway. It was my lovers and I's. Or was it Lovers since there was more than one of them. I honestly did not know. But you know what; I could honestly tell you this. I was in love with at least one man and one beast. Which one would come out on top? No one knows!

Chapter 8

In the early morning sun I awoke to birds chirping, my beautiful body lay neatly in the covers, and my hair was for once not a mess, and when I brushed it, it had no tangles in it. I walked into the kitchen and there was Zeban cooking eggs and bacon.
"Would you like some?" He asked.
"Sure thanks." I said.
I could smell the bacon frying. Kerri came in and handed me a note. I opened it. It was from my secret admirer.

To my love,
Meet me by the two trees at the West end of your building
Love always,
Your Secret Admirer.

I was thrilled finally my secret admirer wanted to meet. I was going to see him for the first time. I became so happy; I started jumping up and down. Every time I jumped up I heard a beep-beep. I stopped and looked around. There was a beeping sound going off. It was a smoke detector. I looked up at the smoke detector, nothing. But the sound kept going off. I looked around at both Kerri and Zeban, they didn't even notice.
I opened my eyes, I was in bed. It had all been a dream. The smoke alarm was going off in the kitchen and even from my room I could smell burnt bacon. I got up and went into the kitchen were Zeban was cursing at the frying pan.
"Is everything ok in here?" I asked.
"It's just fine!" Zeban snapped.
He scrapped the bottom of the pan and walked over to the trash can to throw away the burnt bacon.
"WAIT!" I heard Kerri yell from behind me.
I turned around and there she was.
"I'll eat it!" She said.
"But it's burnt!" I said.
"I don't care!" She said taking the bacon Zeban had just put on a plate.
"You know having her here is just like having a dog! We don't have to worry about throwing away any food!" Zeban said.
I smiled and walked back into my room. I looked in the mirror as I walked by.
"Oh my god!" I said. My hair looked like shit. It was going to take at least an hour to get all these tangles out. I went and laid back down on my bed. I think I preferred the dream!

As I laid in bed I received a surprise. There was a knock at the door. Since I was in my room and Zeban was trying to figure out how to cook bacon without burning it, Kerri answered it. It was my mother.
"Aurroara, your mother is here!" Kerri yelled from the living room.
"I could have done that!" My mother said.
"Then next time maybe you should!" Kerri said and walked away.
My mother was about to give her a good scolding for back talking an elder when I came out of my room.
"Hi mom. I wasn't expecting to see you today!" I said.
"I know, but your father said I can't have a new patio set until I give the old one to a needy family. So I am giving it to you!" She said.
"Ummm, mother you just bought that patio set last year, how can it be old?" I asked.
"Do you want it or not?" She replied.
"Hell ya! Let me get Zeban and Kerri to help take it out of the truck." I said.
"No need I have Dakin with me." She said.

Dakin got out of the truck. I watched as he transformed into a dragon. It was beautiful. He was red from his head to the middle of his shoulders, and then the red started getting darker. From bright red, to maroon, to burgundy, to blood red, to a point were black and red mixed, then to black. It was just gorgeous. He picked up the patio furniture from out of the truck and arranged it as I showed him were to put it. After he was done he changed back to a human and we sat there in my new patio furniture. I loved it. There was a glass table with five chairs. The chairs were all cushioned and looked great. The table had an umbrella in the middle of it. We opened it up and sat in the shade of it. Mom didn't sit long, because she needed to go get her new patio furniture. She took Dakin with her because she needed him to load it in her truck. So I sat there alone for five minutes, when Kerri came out. Kerri being an ex-vampire still could not be in sun light, but she could be in the shade. She sat in one of the chairs next to me.
"I never asked you about that box of chocolates. I saw the card. Who is silver back? She asked me.
"What were you doing in my room, going through my stuff?" I asked.
"Actually I was in the living room and Ramses drug it out. I went to put it back into your room and it fell open. So being the nosey person I am I read it." She explained.
"Oh.Ummm, he is just a friend." I said.
"Aurroara, you're a horrible liar. Is he another admirer?" She asked.
"More of an animal play mate I want a relationship with." I said.

I then told her the story of my silver back. I was going to keep it to myself, but she already knew too much. I had to choose. Tell her the story or kill her and hide the body. Honestly I didn't want to have to carry 350 pounds of human flesh around, dig a hole, and bury it! So I choose to tell her.
"Have you heard from your 'Secret Admirer' lately?" She asked.
"Not since I got the cat." I said.
"Nice, you know if a guy was to send me something I think I would want a chocolate covered cheesecake." She said.
"I would love to get a Lotus Blossom. They are from Egypt and one would have to have them imported. They are not cheap, but they are beautiful!" I said.

Me and Kerri sat out there till it started to get dark, I went inside and got my clothes I have dubbed "The Expandables" and headed for the park. As I got to the park I took off my clothes and hid them in the tree where I usually left them and I felt myself change. I looked around my 'Silver back' was no were to be seen, and that was saying something considering I had perfect eye sight. I jumped up to the tallest building I could find and started running. I leapt from building to building. It felt exhilarating leaping at those heights. Then, there he was. He was standing on one of the buildings in front of me. He stood there waiting for me to run by. When I did he just took one gigantic leap from the building he was on to a nearby building I was now on. Then he took off running. He caught up to me within seconds. We ran till we came to a gap ware the buildings parted to make way for an alley that was big enough to fit the Titanic. My 'Silver back' jumped first. Then I jumped. From ten stories up the jump scared the shit out of me, but I landed on the ground coming to a slide slightly to my left. We stood there starring at one another. Then he walked closer to me and took my paw and kissed me on the lips. A human kiss. In that moment both our faces changed to human. I opened my eyes after he kissed me and for the first time I saw the human behind my 'Silver back'. I was too surprised that I knew him. It was my next door neighbor. I stepped back a few inches. I think he thought I was afraid of him, because he gave me a look of confusion and then hurt. I saw him change back to his werewolf state and start to walk away. I grabbed his paw. I walked closer to him and put my arms around him and pulled him to the ground. There we lay and starred at the stars. I knew as he did we were bound to one another, by love, happiness, animal instinct and fur (A LOT OF FUR)
The next day I awoke in my clothes that I had left in my tree in the park. My 'Silver back' must have carried me back and dressed me then left me here. I smiled and headed for home. When I got there, I found a lotus blossom in a multicolored vase on the doorstep, along with a note.

This is for you! My Egyptian Goddess!

Your Secret Admirer!

I looked at it and was too surprised. I didn't know how to tell this guy whom I was deathly interested in that I was dating a werewolf, and a hot one at that. How does one tear themselves apart. I can have my werewolf, my 'Silver back' and be with one of my own kind; or I could meet my secret admirer and find out if he is the one I want to be with. I was confused and lost. I guess I would have to meet this secret admirer before I could make a decision.

I went to bed and fell back to sleep for a couple of hours. I was awakened about four hours later by a knock on my bedroom door.

"Come in!" I said.

It was Kerri. She came in.

"Hey there is a really hot guy here, who says he knows you, but he doesn't know your name. I think he is our neighbor." She said.

I sprung out of bed and ran to my vanity mirror.

"Tell him I will be out in a minute!" I said.

I got all cute and beautiful. I then walked out into the living room. My neighbor was sitting on the couch opposite Kerri.

"Let's go sit on the patio." I said.

Him and I walked out to the patio and sat down.

"I guess I should introduce myself. My name is Connor. I have been a werewolf for about 150 years." He started.

I guess he saw my look go from interested to "WOW", cause he laughed.

"Ya, I am pretty old. I got changed when I went out riding my horse one night with my wife. We decided to take a moon lit night ride. We rode though the bushes, when something spooked her horse and she was thrown. I stopped my horse and rode over to her. She was ok, a few bumps and bruises. I helped her up and we both got onto my horse. When a huge animal had come out of know where and attacked us. The huge animal was a bear. It had been caught off guard by a werewolf. The werewolf came back and tried to help us, but it went to hit the bear, and hit me instead. The bear killed my wife. There werewolf left. The next full moon I changed into a werewolf for the first time." He finished explaining.

I took his hand "I am sorry to hear about your loss." I said.

"It is 150 years later and I still miss her, but I am ready to move on. That's why I choose you. You are like me. New to it, but the same. Which reminds me, how did you like the Lotus blossom?" He asked.

I looked up stunned.

"Wait, you're my secret admirer?" I asked.

"Yes! Why would a guy keep leaving you gifts on someone else's door step?" He asked.
"I just assumed he was an idiot!" I said.
Connor smiled. He had a wonderful smile. It was soft and bright. He reached over and kissed me. He had soft lips and I liked how they felt on my lips.
"I love you." I said in less than a whisper.
"What?" He said.
"I love it!" I said, trying to pretend I didn't say what I just said.
"I'm glad to hear that." He said.
That night we ran as one. We were more than a couple, more than two werewolves, we were in love.

Chapter 9

My life was finally on the track I had hoped for. I had the man of my dreams.......uhhhhh strike that the animal of my dreams. My roommate Zeban had finally stopped annoying me about me chewing up his shoes and Kerri my other roommate stopped eating me out of house and home (that would be because she went to spend the week with her friend Julie). I was in heaven! My nightly meetings with Connor were sheer bliss. We would run and be free. I loved the way he would hold me and touch me. I wanted him forever. My job was going great, it was summer and the kids were starting the summer reading program. It was where they got prizes for reading. I liked it because it kept the kids busy and away from me. We hadn't had any more bad instances, yet! I was blissfully happy! Too bad it was to be short lived!

On the night of the full moon in the end of June I took myself to the park and got myself ready for the transformation and Connor. The moon came out and I transformed. I started to run, in my peripheral vision I saw another werewolf run up beside me and run with me. Me and him ran like always side by side and racing each other to the edge of the town, were the meadow laid waiting for us. I jumped over him and grabbed him by the middle and flipped him over. I expected him to try and flip my back, but he didn't. We both ended up sliding into the dirt on our sides. (And before you ask, YES, it did hurt!) I got up and walked over to him. He was lying on his side in the dirt, his back to me. He was covered in dirt, his hair color not showing. I walked over and kneeled down beside him to make sure he was ok. When he looked at me his green eyes were the dead giveaway that this was not Connor! I stepped back and starred. The werewolf starred right back! I could see a sly smile crossing his face. And in that moment I knew that he had done this on purpose. His motive, unknown..... At this time! He got up, and once again I found myself being towered over by a male werewolf.

"You know when god was handing out tall pills; he didn't give any to the female werewolves!" I thought to myself.

The green eyed werewolf came closer to me and grabbed my hand. He kissed me using his K-9 mouth and his teeth cut into my lips. I in turn kicked him in his "Charlie Browns" He started to howl, but he kept kissing me. I pushed myself from him, but he grasped me harder to his chest. I kicked and clawed, but I saw in his eyes that he was laughing at me. I became angry and used the anger I was feeling for this asshole to get me out of my situation. I picked him up and threw him across the meadow. I then hunched down on all fours ran over and jumped on top of him holding him down, he tried to overpower me, but I dug my back claws into the ground. I held him there and punched him in the face, in doing so I scratched him under his left eye. I looked at the scratch it was in the shape of an E, it started to bleed. Ya it is going to be a scar.

"I win!" I screamed, Which by the way came out as a loud roar!

I released the idiot and he ran off. I turned and headed toward my park near my home! I was just topping the hill when I saw Connor. He was standing next to the tree were I put my clothes. I watched as the morning sun touched his body and his silver turned to normal skin. I ran down to the tree, hoping no one was watching the nude, crazy lady in the park. When I got there he didn't look happy.

"Hey." I said.

Nothing, not a "Hi", not a "Hey" back....absolute silence. I had done something wrong. I always knew when I had done something wrong, because when I did, my mother would give me the silent treatment, I hated it.

I looked at him.

"What's going on Connor?" I asked as I was putting on my clothes

"I'm leaving. "He said.

"Ok where are you going?" I asked.

"I am going to Utah, I have....I have... I have a daughter there I have to go see!" He said.

"Ok when will you be back?" I asked.

"I am not sure when I am coming back!" He said.

"What? Why not?" I asked.

"I just have to go!" He said as he walked away.

And in that moment, in those 5 words my heart broke. I lost all will to care, live, love or hope. I wanted to die!

I ran home, into my room and cried. For days I transformed and cried in my room, never leaving it. I couldn't believe the man I loved left me to die here on my own. I wanted him back. I wanted him to come to me and tell me it was all a bad dream. To tell me it was a mistake, but the only thing to come to me were the tears. Everything reminded me of him; it was hard not think of him. Hard to do anything. I started trying to do other things to forget him, like find guys online. Maybe if I started dating his memory would disappear. I dated a couple of guys, but every time I was with them, I would sit there and compare them to him, or I would close my eyes and think of him. Then open them expecting him to be there see the other guy and be disappointed. This was becoming harder to deal with.

Finally a week later I went back to work. My fellow employees could see that there was a problem, but thankfully no one asked. I didn't think I could keep my tears in. As long as no one asked me about him I was ok.

At the end of July the full moon came again. When I went out I ran to the meadow. I was hoping for some reason, that maybe he would be there. But it was empty. I sat there, starring at the moon light, when a movement out of the corner of my eye made me jump up. It was the werewolf I had tangled with that one night. I could tell by the E shaped scar under his left eye. I looked at him. He got on all four, showing he was submitting to me. I looked at him unsure what to do, and then I walked over and bowed my head showing him it was ok for him to get up. He walked up to me and licked my face. This made me feel better than I had been feeling. I sat back down and looked back up at the moon. I expected my new werewolf friend to take off, but he sat down next to me. As we sat there he moved closer, then closer, then closer. The next thing I knew he was right next to me and I had put my head on his shoulder. I didn't even realize I was crying until he put his arm around my shoulder and hugged me. We sat there till morning, and I woke up lying next to him. As I got up off the ground he did as well.

"Hi, my name is Jamie." He said.

"My name is Aurroara." I said.

"You looked really sad last night. Are you ok?" He asked.

"No, but I will be. I think! Thanks for being there." I said.

"Not a problem, not like I had anywhere else to go!" He said.

I smiled.

"Hey if you're not busy today, would you like to go have lunch. I know this great little restaurant down by the library. I'd love to take you." He said.
"Sorry I'm busy for lunch!" I said.

"Oh ok!" He said.

"How about dinner?" I asked.

"That sounds great!" He said with a bright smile.

I was feeling better than I had in a while. Connor was still gone and I was still going insane because of it. I missed him so much, but maybe Jamie could help fill the hole that Connor created. Right now I think my biggest problem is going to be how to get home naked without anyone seeing me in broad day light.

Chapter 10

I was happy that I had a new friend in my life. I was still feeling the effects of abandonment from Connor, and I wasn't taking it well. I would hide myself in the house unless I had to work, or wolf-out! And now Jamie was helping me get out even more. The first night we went out to a little Chinese restaurant next to the library. Most people would have called the date a disaster; I called it "A good time!" We got to the restaurant (which is a buffet). So I went to get my plate of food after I told the waitress I wanted a coke. Jamie did the same. I put a couple of things on my plate and came back. Jamie had to wait for them to bring out more beef and broccoli, because yours truly took the last bit! I went and sat down at the table. He came over a little while later and sat his plate on the table, while he was sliding it on the table he looked over his shoulder to ask the waitress for more napkins and pushed his plate into my drink which spilt all over me. I leapt up from the cold ice and soda now spilling down my front. In his hast Jamie tried to reach over to me to help, only to trip the waiter that was cleaning a nearby table causing him to spill leftover food from his cleaning tray on to me! I was now doused in coke, sweet and sour sauce, and all kinds of god only knows what. Then a couple was too busy starring at me on their way out to notice that their baby that the husband was carrying dropped its ice cream in my hair. I stood there not really knowing how to react to this turn of events. I started to laugh as I saw Jamie's face, his look was one of crap I am going to have to transform and stop her when she transforms and tears this place apart. As I laughed Jamie started laughing. I went into the bathroom cleaned the egg role, and bits of other food out of my hair and off my cloths. Then got some napkins and dried up some of the other soda, sauces and soups that were on me. I went back in to the restaurant and the waitress had moved Jamie to another table and we finished having dinner after getting fresh plates of food.

After dinner Jamie walked me home. While standing at my doorway he starred at me.

"You are so beautiful, Aurroara!" He said.

"Thank you! I really appreciate that." I said.

He had no idea how much exactly I really, really needed to hear that after Connor.

Jamie kissed me on the check and left. I felt a hot glow on my check were he kissed me and smiled. I think I was beginning to feel better.

The next day I went to work feeling better then, I had in days. I did no longer want to hide in my room. I know I wasn't in love with Jamie, but I was in lust. I got to work and opened the library. There were not a lot of people in the morning so things went rather smoothly, until about 12:15pm. I was sitting at the front desk when a raving mother came in and asked me why she got a bill for a book her daughter never returned.

"Let me pull up her account." I said.

The woman stood there until I pulled up the account.

"The title of the book is Love and Life by: Emma Pluto" I said.

"The woman looked at me, my daughter never checked out that book I did....ummm how much is the fine?" She asked politely.

"It is 32.50 because the book was never brought back." I said.

"Yes, let me pay that right now." She said.

"That's right, don't be blaming us for your mistake, bitch!" I thought to myself with a smile.

That was as dangerous as my day got, but it got a whole lot happier when I saw Jamie walk in. I watched as he walked to the new DVD's and selected "Sherlock Holmes" with Robert Downey Jr. He walked up to me.

"Hi!" He said.

"Hi, how can I help you?" I asked trying to be professional.

"I would like to check this movie out." He said.

"I can do that for you." I said and took the movie and scanned his library card, then scanned the movie.

"Have you seen this movie before?" He asked.

"No, but I do want to!" I lied. I have seen it like a billion times, who wouldn't want to see Robert Downey Jr.? He is a hottie!!!!
"How about you come over tonight and watch it with me?" He asked.

"Seriously?" I asked before I could stop myself.

He looked at me surprised.

"I'm sorry, I meant what time." I said, as I recovered myself

"What time do you get off?" He asked.

"I get off at 6pm tonight." I said.

"Let's make it 7pm, then." He said.

"That sounds great. Would you like me to bring anything?" I asked.

"Nope, just yourself." he said with a sly smile.

I smiled and handed him his movie. He reached out put his hand on mine and took the movie, leaving his hand behind touching me. I didn't want him to go, I was about to leap over the counter, grab him by his shirt and kiss him, when he looked into my eyes and said

"I'll see you tonight." and left.

"You know, sometimes I really hate being a librarian! I can't stripe, I can't kick noisy little children, and I can't leap over the counter and make out with a really hot guy. What's the matter with this world?" I thought to myself.

Chapter 11

I went home after work intent on getting ready for my movie date with Jamie, only to find a house full of cheese (of all things). I looked around the wheels of cheese and the brown bags of cheese from everywhere in the world. I made my way through the cheese that was crowding my living room and found my way to the dining room.

"Hey you, when did you get home?" I asked Kerri.

"About an hour ago. Julie was annoying the hell out of me." She said.

"Uhuh.....and...." I said waiting for her to explain the cheese.

"What?" She said.

"The cheese Kerri, were did all this cheese come from?" I asked.

You know there are times when one asks a question, one really wishes they had worded better. This was one of those times.

"The man with the truck dropped it off; I think he said it was made in Michigan!" She said.
"Kerri, you're an idiot! Did it come with any papers, cards, notes....anything to explain where it came from and who sent it, and most importantly, who it is for?" I said.

"Oh you want that info. The paper work he gave me is under that." She said and pointed to a very large wheel of Gouda.

I walked over and picked up the cheese with one hand and found a packet of papers underneath it. I picked them up and put the cheese back down. I walked into my room with the papers. In it I found a card:

"I know you love cheese and I love you, hope you understand!"

Was all it said! I knew it was from Connor. He was the only one I told about my obsession with cheese. I love cheese. I love trying new cheeses.

"Ya, I understand you ditched me and ran off!" I said out loud.

It had been about 2 months since I had heard from Connor and all though this gift was absolutely wonderful and extremely expensive, I still was angry for him ditching me and leaving. I guess I was angrier at the fact that he didn't give me a reason he just left. I put the paper work down and started to get ready for my date with Jamie.

At 7:05 I was ready.

"Ya I was late! But gorgeous people have that privilege! And I am ubber gorgeous!" I said to myself. I then walked out into the living room.

"Wow you look good!" Kerri said.

"Thank you!" I said.

I stood there about to walk out the door, when I had an extremely great idea. I grabbed multiple different types of cheeses and cut them into cubes. I then put them on a plate with some crackers I had and put saran wrap on it. I then walked out the front door and got into my car. I drove down the street. When I pulled up to Jamie's apartment I double checked my makeup and hair in the pull down mirror. "Ya I looked gooooooood!" I said to myself.

I grabbed the cheese tray and walked up to the door. With a big breathe I knocked. Nothing. I knocked again. Nothing. I stood there for a minute, and then knocked again. I looked at my watch, 7:30pm. I didn't know what to do. I didn't have his phone number I forgot to ask for it. I opened my purse and took out the note pad I received as a gift for Librarians Week. I wrote a note to Jamie.

"Hey you, I came by for our date.....I crossed off date....our movie...time...thingy...Anyway you weren't here. So I am leaving this note. But I guess you already know I am leaving this note since you are reading it. Anyway call me!

I left my number on the note as well. I started to walk back down the hall to the parking lot. I got to my car, when a car pulled up beside me and rolled down its windows.

"Hey sexy, where do you think you're going?" Jamie said from inside the car.

"Well since your here I might just stay and watch a movie." I said.

"Sorry about that, I ran out to get us some soda. I thought we might want something to go with the popcorn." He said.

"Awww that was so thoughtful." I said.

"Have you been waiting long?" He asked.

"Crap," I thought. "Ok I can lie and say yes, I was waiting here since 7pm, and he might not have left till 7:15 and he would know I was lying. Or I could tell him the truth that I was running late and I just got here." I decided to go with the later.

"No I was running late, so I just got here." I said.

"Super, then it works out good." He said.

He grabbed his groceries and together we carried our stuff into his apartment. I walked in and the scent of men's cologne hit me. It wasn't over powering; it was just there to let you know there was a man that lived here. I carried my stuff into the kitchen and set it on the counter next to the stuff he just set down. I then walked into the living room and set down on the couch. Jamie came in a little while later with the platter of cheese and crackers, soda and some popcorn. He put the movie in the DVD player and we sat there him on the left end of the couch me on the right for the duration of the movie (Which is 2 hours and 8 minutes). Finally when the movie was over we turned to each other.

"What are you thinking, right now?" He asked.

"Nothing." I said.

"Really..." He said moving down the couch to my side.

"Really, really!" I said. I moved closer to him, to meet him in the middle instead of making him come all the way to my side.

"How long have you been a werewolf?" I asked, trying to break the silence.

"For about 75 years. It hasn't been easy, let me tell you." He said.

"I bet. I am only a couple of months old." I said.

"Ya, I heard!" He said.

"Really, what else did you hear?" I asked trying to be seductive.

"You know just gossip really." He said and then he leaned over and kissed me.

"What kind of relationship are you looking for?" I asked him wondering if he wanted a relationship with me or just friends.

"Well now that Connor is out of the picture I can have you all to myself. Why don't we...." He didn't get to finish.

"What do you mean Connor is out of the picture. How do you know Connor? And how do you know we had a relationship?" I asked.

"Seriously?" he asked.

I gave him the "Yes! I am very serious" look.

"Well, Connor and I have been rivals ever since he changed me. I have taken every woman he has ever been with. I think it was good revenge for what he did to me!" He said.

"But I don't understand, Connor left before me and you started dating!" I said.

"He left because he saw, the scene I wanted him to see! You on top of me, in the moon light, in the meadow!" He said.

I thought back to the first night of when Jamie had first attacked me.

"It was all a game, a ploy to get Connor to leave. He saw me and you that night and just assumed you and me were......what the hell?" I screamed at him as I pushed him away from me and got up.

"What, you would never be happy with him. I am what you want!" He said.

"Wrong, you don't understand Jamie. I fell in love with Connor. And Hell has no fury like a woman scorned. And you took my lover away from me, that my dear is a scorn that will get you killed." I said. I became angry and in my rage I lunged at Jamie and punched him in the face, he fought back, but my anger over powered anything he tried to throw at me. I had him down on the ground.

"Listen to me Jamie, you have exactly 24 hours to get him back, or I will make you pay! Do you understand?" I said.

Jamie saw the anger in my eyes and I think for the first time ever, feared someone other than himself.

"Fine, I will try!" He said.

I got up and grabbed my cheese tray, dumped it on Jamie's head and walked out. As I drove home I listened to "I'd come for you by: Nickleback" and thought of Connor.

Will he come back, if I ask him to? Or will his pride keep him away? I was sad again, but this time I knew there was a way to fix it, I just had to find out how!

Chapter 12

I awoke in my bed to a scream coming from the other side of my door. I jumped up and ran in to the living room. I stood there and studied the scene before me. There was Kerri holding on to the end of what looked like a rare steak. And holding on to the other end was Ramses, my cat.

"Ummm, what's going on Kerri?" I asked.

"Your little feline friend is trying to steal my steak! He is NOT getting it!" She declared.

"Why don't you just tell him to drop it?" I asked.

Kerri looked at me.

"Drop it!" She screamed at Ramses.

He gave her a, 'whatever look!'

"Ramses drop it!" I said and walked back into my room.

Ramses dropped the steak, bit Kerri on the leg and followed me in to my room.

"I'll get you some steak from the store today. That isn't tainted with Kerri's germs. ok?" I said.

Ramses gave me an affectionate smile and lick. (I see kitty licks, as kisses.)

"Awww my kitty loves me!" I said to Ramses. He looked at me with the look on his face that said "Really, you seriously think I like you. No, you feed me and house me so I have to tolerate you, but that's it!"
I started to laugh.

I got up and got dressed for work. I choose my sleek black pants and shiny black top. I looked good, as always!
I walked into the kitchen and got some pieces of watermelon, some cheese and some regular chips for breakfast. I ate at the table in my room and watched tv

while I ate. After my fiesta breakfast, I got in my car and drove to work. When I got there I noticed everyone was staring at me. They all smiled and grinned as if they knew something I didn't.

"And how are we today?" Hellzone asked me.

"Umm, fine! What's going on?" I asked.

"What do you mean?" He asked.

"Seriously? Hellzone everyone here is acting funny, what's going on?" I asked.

He smiled at me and walked me to the front desk. There next to the wall, was a fantastic bouquet of red roses, and in the center was an Egyptian Lotus blossom (which was blue).

"Wow it's beautiful!" I said.

“It's for you.” Hellzone stated.

"What? For me? Are you serious?" I asked.

"Yep, came this morning. We know it's for you because the name on card is yours!" He said.

I walked over to the bouquet. I smelled them. They were fresh, and gorgeous. I lifted the card. Opened it and read it:

Rose are red, Lotus blossoms are blue, I want you to know that I love you!

Signed Your Secret Admire (You know who!)

It was from Connor!

"Wow! Jamie sure did work fast. He got to Connor within 24 hours. He must be really afraid I was going to hurt him!" I thought.

"I wonder if that means he is here in town." I asked myself.

"No, it would take longer for him to get here!" I answered myself.

I went to work at the H desk. I sat there wondering where Connor was and what he was doing. I become so involved in my thoughts that when a woman came up to me and asked for a library card I didn't answer right away. In fact I didn't answer for a couple of minutes. It took Hellzone touching me on the arm, to bring me out of my daze to actually come back. The rest of the day went by smoother, I tried to keep myself busy and not think about Connor. This turned out to be harder than I anticipated. But when there was a loud bang that came from the back of the library it gave me something to inquire about. I walked back to the back corner with Hellzone, stood there while he talked to two young boys who started fighting. I got bored and decided to go back up to the front to see if anyone needed help; I didn't think anyone stayed up there to help the patrons. As I got the front desk I was correct, all the staff had gone to the back of the library to see what was going on. As I walked around the corner to the back side of the H desk, I noticed a young man playing with the cash register.

"Can I help you?" I asked.

He starred at me, not knowing really what to say at first.

"Yes, I am the son of the library manager and he wants to know why, you're not in the back helping the other employees?" He stated.

I looked him up and down and laughed.

"Hon, first off our manager has NO kids, secondly even if she did, they would know NOT to touch the register. And thirdly our manager likes to yell at us personally, she doesn't send others to do it for her, and fourthly our manager is a SHE!" I said, my voice getting louder and louder with every number I said.

The boy turned red, and reached out to hit me. I grabbed his arm, turned it around behind his back and lowered him to the floor. Where I sat on him till Hellzone showed up.

"Ummm, Aurroara, why are you sitting on a patron?" He asked.

"This patron," I pointed to the one I was sitting on. "was trying to break into the cash register. I am guessing that his friends in the back were just a diversion." I explained.

"Really, great work Aurroara, pinning him down!" Hellzone said.

"Thanks!" I said, getting up and letting Hellzone take him into the back as I called the police.

I got back on the H desk and got on my email. Ok I have like 5 different email address.

One is for job hunting,(just in case I need a second job!)

Another is for man hunting. (If I meet a guy and want to give him my email address.)

Another is for my Avon job,(I am trying.)

Another is one I have had for about 15 years that all my old friends know.

And the last one is for everything else.

The one I have had for 15 years I hadn't checked in about 3-4 months, I opened it and there were 11472 emails in it! I was flabbergasted and a little bit over whelmed. I started reading the emails and didn't even notice that 3 hours had gone by and it was time for me to go to lunch. I decided to have Chinese, and to go by myself since last time it was a bit of a mess. I ate lunch/dinner by myself and loved every minute. It was quite and gave me time to think, and was cheaper than paying for two. When I got back to work it was slow and quite. I decided I had had enough of emails for one day, so I didn't even bother opening any of my emails. I sat there for two hours at 8pm, we started our closing list. We have a list because it is really long and it helps to remember what needs to get done. We started the list and at 830, we were half way done. At 845 we had done everything except close and lock the doors, so we sat at our desks and waited till 9pm. I was sitting there looking at new books that had come out; when someone came in. I didn't bother to look up, because I wanted to finish looking at the list. But whoever it was came to the H desk and I had to help them.

"Hi can I help you?" I said without looking up.

Nothing, there was no answer. So I looked up and into the sparkling green eyes of Connor.

My heart just burst and I wanted to jump over the counter and kiss him and hold him. But I didn't!

"Hello, can I help you?" I asked again, this time looking him straight in the eyes. He smiled at me.

"Yes, it seems. I am a complete ass-hole. I saw something a few months ago and assumed I knew what it was. Turns out I was wrong. I should have asked, but I didn't, and I ran. Do you have any books that help with, I am sorry, I'm an idiot, please forgive me?" He asked.

I looked at him.

"Nope!" I stated out loud.

A surprise look came over his face and he turned and started walking away.

I jumped over the counter and landed on my feet in front of him,

"But I do have books on there's nothing to forgive, and I love the flowers!" I said with a smile.

He smiled and kissed me.

Chapter 13

Connor and I spent the entire night at my house eating cheese and watching movies. In the middle of our movie fest, my mother called. (Ya that was a mood breaker!)

"Aurroara, I have proof I have a stalker!" My mother announced after I answered my phone.

"Really mother and what is this proof?" I asked her.

"Well last night, which by the way was not a full moon; so don't try to tell me it was you and your transformation skills." She said.

"Ummm, ok sure. What are you talking about?" I asked.

"Well last night, I left me shoes outside the door. Because I knew you weren't going to be out. So I put them out. Well when I woke up this morning, they had been shredded and put into a heart shape!" She explained.

"Really?" I asked.

"Yes, I told your father, but he said I was just being paranoid and that I should put up a camera to catch them on film." She said.

"Ok, so why are you calling me?" I asked.

"Do you have a camera I can borrow?" She asked.

"Yes, I got one from AVON; do you want to come get it?" I asked.

"Yes, I will send your father for it tomorrow." She said then hung up.

"Ummm, wow good to talk to you too!" I said out loud to my phone.

"What's going on?" Connor asked, from the couch.

"Nothing, just my mother being crazy, that's all!" I said as I sat back down with him.

At that very moment Kerri came out of the bathroom, it was about 10:30pm.

"Hey you!" She said.

"Hey, what's up?" I asked.

"Nothing much, just getting ready for my class." She said.

"Which class are you taking this semester?" I asked.

"Well, I am taking Pharmacy 101, Algebra 115, Reading 208, English 121, and yoga." She said.

"Wow, that's a lot of classes!" Connor said.

"Ya. I take a lot of classes because I get bored really fast. And yoga I take because I get stressed out really fast as well!" She said with a laugh.

"Well, what classes are tonight?" I asked.

"Algebra and yoga!" She said.

"Cool, well have fun!" Connor said.

"I will, oh hey Aurroara, Zeban said he will be gone for the next two weeks and not to chew up his shoes!" Kerri recited from her memory.

"Ummm, ok where did he go?" I asked.

"To see his mother, it's a burning day sometime this week and he wants to be there for her before and after." She said, and then she walked out the door.

"I guess we are alone!" I stated.

"Yes, just you, me and the cheese." Connor said with a laugh.

I slid over and lay in his arms.

"Can I ask you a really odd question?" He asked.

"Sure, what? I asked back.

"What's up with your room mate, Kerri. What's her story?" He asked.

"Well it's kind of a long story!" I said.

"I have know where to go!" He said.

"Ok, well Kerri had been a vampire since god, 1800's I think. Somewhere about that time. She was a loner, never really settling down. She was thin, kind of looked like Zoe Saldana, you know the girl who played Uhura from the new 'StarTrek' movie. She went from town to town feeding off the blood of humans. Sometimes killing them, sometimes turning them. Not really caring. Then in 1982, she was walking through the forest when she came upon some campers. She attacked them and was sucking the blood from the last one, when a bear snuck up on her and ripped the shit out of her. A young hiker named Dwight, came upon her and assumed she was a survivor from the bear attack that killed the others. Which is not true she did, but anyway. He drug her to his house and cared for her and got her back to health. He figured out, that she was a vampire. I think it was the fact that she kept throwing up all the food he gave her. So he started giving her his blood, and freshly killed animals to feed off of. Kerri fell in love with him. They would spend nights were he would just watch her for hours, and she would lay next to him watching him. They connected and loved each other. One night Kerri was up stairs, when Dwight called her to come down stairs. She came down to a candle filled room and a special dinner on the table. He walked her over to the couch and sat her down.

"We have been together for 5 years. And I love being with you. I want you to be with me forever. Will you marry me?" He asked.

Kerri was ecstatic. She loved him more than anything in the world.

"But before you answer, I have one request. Will you become like me, a vampire?" She asked.

He looked into her eyes, "Of course, I will!" He said.

She looked into his eyes. "Of course, I will" She said.

They kissed, but while they were kissing a gang of vampires broke into Dwight's house. Not knowing that Kerri was already a vampire, they sucked her blood not killing her; but weakening her. She blacked out. When she awoke she found

Dwight dead with the ring in his hands. She vowed never to drink human blood again. She survived on animals until in 1998 she came across the company that made the synthetic blood and started getting that from them. Then the synthetic blood made her gain ubber amounts of weight and she just never cared to get rid of it. Dwight was dead, and she didn't want to give her heart to anyone else." I finished.

"Wow, that's really sad." He said.

"Ya, I know how she feels, kind of." I said.

"Really, why?" He asked.

"Shit, shit, shit....." I thought to myself.

"Ummm, so do you want some cheese?" I asked about to get up, he pulled me back down.

"Why won't you tell me?" He asked looking into my eyes.

His green eyes became loving and I just sank into him.

"I thought I was going to die, when you left. I...I...I..." I stammered, I didn't want to tell him, I had fallen in love with him.

He looked in my eyes.

"You know I have fallen in love with you, right!" He said.

"My entire life just became livable!" I thought.

"I love you to, Connor!" I said.

Then he kissed me ever so passionately.

I awoke on the couch alone. I looked on the table and there was a note taped to a knife that was stuck into a wheel of Gouda Cheese. The note said:

I will be by tonight to see you. I had a wonderful time last night. Can't wait to see you!

Love always, Connor

I was absolutely delighted.

"I wonder what he went to go do." I thought to myself.

I went into my room, and lay down, it was Wednesday and I was off today. A day I could just do nothing. My cat came in and licked my hand, as if to ask me, did you pick up my steak?

"Oh I'm sorry Ramses, I forgot your steak, but here I'll make a deal with you. I will give you a small cube of cheese, and go buy you some steak! How does that sound?" I asked him, as if he was going to answer. I guess he did in his own way. He bit my hand, swished his tail in my face, jumped off the bed and looked back at me as if to say, "Well where the hell is my cheese!"

I got off the bed and cut him a small piece of cheese and gave it to him. He seemed content. I went to my room and got dressed, god forbid my diva of a cat not get his steak!

I went down to the super market and went inside. It was nice, the outside it was hot, but there was air conditioning inside, so I was nice and cool! I walked down the meat isle and looked at the steak. I was looking at a rather nice t-bone for me and a small sirloin for Ramses, when I was tapped on the shoulder. I turned around and there was my brother.

"Hey little bro, what's up?" I asked.

"Nothing much!" He said.

"What are you doing here, I thought Nama did the shopping?" I asked.

"Ya, she does, but I have to buy some foam!" He said.

At that very moment Sterben ran around the corner,

"Dude, I got some!" He yelled.

"Ummm, what are you guys doing?" I asked.

"Nothing!" They both answered in unison looking away.

"Liars! What are you guys doing?" I asked again, my curiosity peeked.

"Ok, if we tell you, you can't tell mom!" Dewar said.

"Ummm, ok!" I said rather lost.

"Well you know how mom thinks she has a stalker right!" He asked.

"Yes!" I answered.

"Well she doesn't! Me and Sterbin have been stealing her shoes and putting pieces of foam on the matt to make her think someone has been stealing her shoes!" He explained rather happily.

"Ummm, why did you put the pieces in to a heart shape last night?" I asked.

"What are you talking about?" Sterben asked.

"Mom called me last night and said her stalker left her shoe pieces on her mat in the shape of a heart!" I explained.

"Dude, that must have been an accident, because we didn't leave them in any specific shape. But now that she thinks we did, we are so going to leave them in a star pattern tonight!" he said.

"Just out of curiosity, why are you guys doing this?" I asked.

"Just something to do!" Dewar answered.

"Ya, we have been totally bored the last couple of weeks!" Sterben answered.

"Why don't you play video games?" I asked.

"Cause I like being out at night! And video games get boring, they are not real life!" He explained.

"So you go out and destroy our mother's shoes?" I asked.

"No, we steal her shoes and leave pieces of foam we bought. We still have her shoes, we don't destroy anything!" Dewar explained.

"Ok, that's the lamest excuse of something to do I have ever heard!" I said.

"Yes, but it keeps us from going crazy!" Sterben said.

"Whatever!" I said then grabbed my steak and walked away.

"Hey don't tell mom, k!" Dewar yelled out.

"I won't!" I yelled back.

While standing in the line to check out, I had a dilemma. Should I tell my mother about my brother stealing her shoes or not. On one hand I didn't want her thinking she had a stalker, on the other it was just plain funny. So I think I will just let Dewar and Sterbin have their fun. It does give me something to laugh about now that I was in the loop, and mom was going to borrow my camera. She would find out at some point.

Chapter 14

It was going to be the Fourth of July weekend and Mom wanted everyone to come out for a BBQ on July 3rd because it was a Saturday. I thought that this was a great idea, except I had to work.

"Mom, I can't come out to the BBQ this weekend I have to work." I said.

"Aurroara, I ask very few things from my children, and one of them is for you to come to this BBQ!" She said her voice getting louder.

"Well I have to work; I don't get off till 6pm!" I said.

"Aurroara, don't be a dumbass, the party doesn't start till 7pm, cause it doesn't get dark till 8pm and we will be setting off fireworks!" She stated.

"Oh, ok. Then I will be there! Do you want me to bring anything?" I asked.

"Just your famous deviled eggs!" She said.

"Ok, I will bring them." I said and hung up.

I sat there and wondered if I should invite Connor to our little Fourth of July thingy. I wasn't sure if I was ready for my family to intermingle with the werewolf I had fallen in love with. I never told them what had happened between us. When he left and broke my heart I had kept to myself not talking to them much. I didn't want them to see my broken heart. I guess I had felt weak crying like I did, but now I feel they are my feelings and if I want to cry I can and I will!

It was July 1 today, Thursday. I had to get ready for work. Looking for clothes is always an adventure. I am not fashion gifted. My fashion sense consists of black pants and a black top.

"Since that crisis is fixed on to another!" I thought as I finished dressing and walked out to my car.

The drive to work was quite and easy, but as soon as I rounded the corner to the library and saw the 15 police cars I knew the day was not going to be easy. I parked and got out of my car. I walked into the building and saw Hellzone.

"What's going on?" I asked him.

"It seems, some young halogens broke in and stole 5 of our Laptops!" He said.

"Ummm, they are aware that they have tracking devises on them, right?" I asked.

"Apparently not. I have activated the devises and our computer is locating them now!" Hellzone explained.

There was a beeping coming from the computer. It had located them.

"They are located at an address about 10 miles from here!" Hellzone said printing out the address and handing it to the officer.

"Thank you, we will retrieve them for you!" He said.

I walked over and sat at the H desk. Well honestly the four hours I was at the H desk the only thing interesting that happened was Hellzone telling me what happened when the police located the laptops.

"So have you heard anything on the laptops?" I asked

"Yes, oh my goodness I am surprised I haven't told you." He said in a slightly excited tone.

"Ok what?" I asked.

"Well it seems that the police showed up at the house address on the slip of paper I gave them. They knocked and a woman answered the door. The police said they were looking for 5 laptops and had a warrant to search the premises. The woman said no and slammed the door in their faces. SO the police knocked on the door again and told her that if she didn't open the door they were going to break it down. Well she didn't open the door so the broke it down. And inside they found meth lab!" He said.

"Oh my goodness, seriously!!" I said excited.

"Yes, the mother was seriously pissed off with the son for stealing the laptops which he would have only got two thousand dollars for, when they had a meth lab that brought in over 25 thousand a month." He said.

I laughed.

As Hellzone walked away I noticed an 8' foot tall Pegasus/man walk in. He walked over to the H desk with a marvelous bouquet of flowers.

I smiled and felt like an idiot, in front of this really hot Pegasus/man. Which I later learned the species was called Pegamen.

"Those are beautiful!" I said.

"Thank you, they are for a..." He paused as he looked at the delivery slip.

"Aurroara!" He said

"Really, that's me!" I said as I showed him my name tag.

He smiled at me and laughed a little, I felt like an idiot.

I walked around the desk and walked up to him. He towered over me. I looked at the flowers; they were a dozen beautiful Lotus Blossoms. I took the vase and turned around to carry it to the break room, when in my turn I slipped and fell backwards, right on to the Pegaman. He caught me from falling to the floor, but the water and the flowers from the vase went all over me. I laid there in his arms for a minute or two. I was soaked! He gently let me up and water sloshed to the floor. He helped me pick up the flowers and put them back into the vase, and then he carried the vase, and followed me while I walked to the break room. When I got back there I opened up my locker and got my purse, it was time for me to go anyway I might as well go home and change.

I took the flowers from the Pegaman.

"Thank you!" I said.

"You're welcome!" He said.

"I guess I should go home and dry off!" I said.

"Ya, you're pretty soaked!" He said

We stood there for a moment.

"You know there is a better way you can dry off!" He said.

I looked at him questioningly.

He smiled.

"How would you like a ride? The hot air outside will dry your cloths in no time at all!" He said.

I smiled and didn't really know what to say.

"Sounds fun!" I finally said. I put my purse and around my neck and walked with him out the door.

He spread out his wings and in the sun light I could see a beautiful pair of white wings, with gold streaks in them.

"I have never ridden before, how do I get on?" I asked.

He kneeled down and I climb up.

"You ready?" He asked.

"Ummm, before we take off, what's your name?" I asked.

"My name is Desiderio. My friends call me Rio." He said and took off.

We flew through the air just above the roof tops. I saw my house. Then I saw my house getting smaller and smaller. We were going higher. I soon was in the air and the clouds surrounded me. I reached out my hand and touched them. They felt like cotton candy tasted. You put it in your mouth but it melts to fast to chew. Clouds were like this when you touch them, they disappeared to fast to feel them. I was in heaven. He did a loop and I went flying through the air, as he came down from the loop he caught me in his arms. I laughed. I was having a marvelous time. Then something unexpected happened. I was in his arms, when he kissed me. Not really knowing what to do, I kissed him back. I turned my entire body around and secured my legs around his waist and my arms around his neck. We made out in the sky. After a make out session that lasted for an hour, I climbed back on to his back, and we headed back for earth. He landed back at the back entrance of the library.

I smiled at him. Not really knowing what to say.

"I would like to see you again." He said.

"I would like to see you again as well, but..." I said.

"But what?" He said.

"I am kind of seeing this guy." I said.

"Kind of or are?" He said.

"I am not sure, what's going on with it!" I said.

"Well here is my number, give me a call. I would love to do it again!" He said and took off into the sky.

I walked back inside picked up my vase of flowers added some water and straightened them up.

That was when I found the card.

"To my lovely werewolf-ess, I can't wait to hold you, lick you and pet you! LOL werewolf humor! I will see you tonight my love."

"Oh my god, how do I get myself into these messes?" I asked myself.

Chapter 15

I awoke the next morning feeling like I had drunk an entire bottle of vodka and washed it down with dirt. When I opened my eyes and looked at the calendar to what date it was I realized I probably wasn't far off. All be it I had not drank any vodka, or eaten any dirt the previous night, but when having to deal with my family and the guilt of what I had just done with Rio, I might as well have drank a whole bottle of vodka and eaten dirt. Because the consequences of this day were going to be hell!

I drug myself out of bed and walked into the living room, where I was caught off guard by a horrendous sight. At first I didn't know what it was, then my eyes focused and I figured it out. It was Kerri's behind. It wouldn't have been bad, but she was in a thong and tank top. All I could see was two giant butt checks with a thin strip of cloth that started to disappeared, then reappeared somewhere at the bottom.

"Ummm, what are you doing?" I asked closing my eyes so the image could erase itself from my memory.

"I am trying to get my locket from under the couch!" She yelled out.

"I didn't know you had a locket?" I said.

"I do, it's new!" She said.

"Really, cool. Where did you get it? I was thinking about getting one for my mother." I asked.

There was silence. It was like one of those Twix commercials, were the guy says something stupid and he pulls out a Twix to give him a moment to think of a reason of why he said what he said.

"Hello, earth to Kerri!" I said.

"Sorry I found a Twix candy bar under here, I was eating." She said.

"And the locket?" I asked.

"Oh Ya, I got it from a friend as a gift." She said.

"Oh, someone's got a boyfriend; someone's got a boy friend!" I taunted.

"Well he is kinda cute and sexy. And I think he really likes me!" She said.

"I am glad to see you are getting on with your life. Moving on is a very important step in the healing process." I said, sounding like a therapist.

"Thank you doctor Freud!" She said sarcastically as she got up off the floor and gave me the finger.

"This guy is different from all the others. He asks about my life, school, home, me. I tell him everything from what I do at home. To Ramses trying to steal my steak. I even told him about you and the cheese. He was interested in hearing why some guy would send anyone tons of cheese." She said.

"Fun! I am going to have an omelet, with that tons of cheese!" I said.

"No, I'll make you one. I was going to make me one anyways." She said.

I was suspicious.

"What do you want Kerri?" I asked.

"What do you mean?" She asked not looking directly into my eyes.

"Kerri every time you are willing to do anything nice for me like this you want something. What?" I asked.

"Ok, well I was thinking I could invite David and Julie over and we could all sit and get to know him. What do you think?" She asked.
"It's fine with me. Is Zeban back from his mothers?" I asked.

"Ya, he came back last night. Said something about getting bored of her." She said.

"Did you ask him if it was ok if you brought these people over?" I asked.

"Yes, he said to shut the hell up, get the hell out of his room and ask you." She said using quotation fingers.

"Well he certainly has a colorful vocabulary! Who is David?" I asked.

"He's the guy who gave me the locket!" She said

"Oh ok, when did you want to have them over?" I asked.

"How about tomorrow night?" She said excited.

"Ok, right now I have to go get ready for my family's 4th of July celebration. Are you coming out to my parents?" I asked.

"Ya, I will get a ride from Zeban, because I know you want to be alone with your honey on the ride out there!" She said with a smile.

"What are you talking about?" I asked.
"Connor." She said.

"What about him?" I asked.

"He is going out there with you." She said.

"No he's not. He doesn't even know about it." I said.

"Ummm, oops!" I heard Kerri whisper under her breathe.

"What did you do?" I asked using a louder than normal voice.

"Well he called asking to talk to you. I said you were still in bed. He said he would call back later. I said he could just talk to you when you two rode out to your parents for the 4th of July BBQ!" She explained.

I starred at her, not really knowing whether to throw the remote, the chair, or the table at her. Honestly my first thought was to throw the car, but then I calmed down and just breathed.

"When am I supposed to pick him up?" I asked.

"He is going to come over about noon." She said.

I looked at the clock. It was 10:30am. That gave me time enough to take a shower, get ready and make sure I looked good.

"You're lucky I don't slap you!" I said.

"I know, that's why I asked you about having David over first, before I told you I fucked up!" She said.

I honestly had to hold myself back or I was going to slap her. I walked back to my room.

"Hey there is another message for you. A guy brought it to the door." She said.

I ignored her and flopped down on my bed.

"Who is Rio?" She said.

"Oh shit!" I yelled.

I ran to the door grabbed the note from her and closed the door on her face.

I walked back and laid on my bed and read the letter.

To my dearest Lotus Blossom,

Yesterday was absolutely wonderful. I would love to spend the 4th of July evening with you. Let me know, my number is 719-232-1592. Text me at any time. I will be at home.

Yours Truly,

Rio.

"Oh crap." I thought to myself.

I really liked my flight in the clouds with Rio. But I loved Connor. Well at least I think I did. I was really confused. Maybe tonight when I spent the evening with him, it would help me gain more perspective about my feelings for him.

I took a shower and got dressed. I looked wonderful. I walked over to Connor's apartment and knocked on the door. He answered wearing nothing but a towel covering his bottom half. I was breathless. He body was perfect, well I thought so anyway. He grabbed me pulled me into his apartment and closed the door while kissing me. I felt so safe and secure with him. He let me go and told me to wait on the couch while he got dressed. I sat there and looked around his apartment. There wasn't much. A couch and loveseat were against the walls, they made an L shape. A glass table in the middle of the room and a stand with a TV on it. In the corner was a desk, with a lot of papers on it. I was nosey, so I walked over pretending to look at a picture and moved my eyes to the papers. It was a letter from someone called Nightshade. All I could read of it was 'get her, we need her. Our Alliance will need her!' If I moved the paper on top of it, I could have read the rest of it, but Connor walked into the room at that moment.

"That's me and Al Capone." He said.

I didn't know if he was serious or not. I looked at the picture, I was supposed to be looking at anyway and sure enough it was Connor and Al Capone shaking hands.

"He is a very interesting guy. Sorry, was.... an interesting guy. Met him by accident. I was being chased down by some werewolf hunters and I ran into him. He was bootlegging liquor. He shot the hunters and killed them. I had been shot in the leg by one of them and Capone bandaged it and stayed with me till morning. Then when I turned back into a human he helped me back to my car. We became rather good friends. He didn't say anything about what went on in my world at night and I didn't say anything about what he did at night. It was perfect until he landed in Alcatraz prison; he never really recovered from that." He said.

"I'm sorry." I said putting a hand on his shoulder.

We stood in silence, then we walked to the door and out to the car. On the way out to my parents we listened to one of my favorite singers, 'Lady Gaga'. I loved the fact that she just had her own style and did whatever she wanted. My favorite song by her at this moment was 'Dance in the Dark!" As I sang out loud the lyrics Connor reached over and took my hand.

"You have a beautiful voice." He said.

I smiled. After about 15 minutes of driving we reached my mother's house. I opened the gate and drove the car in. I would have let Connor do it, but it was kind of complicated. After I drove the car in I closed the gate behind me and got back in the car and drove it up to the house. Both me and Connor got out of the car. We walked up to the fence and opened the gate. Connor closed it behind us. We walked over to the patio on the side of the house. As soon as we were in view of everyone. There was silence. Everyone stopped talking to find out who the new guy was.

"Everyone, this is Connor." I said.

"Awww is he your werewolf boyfriend?" Sterben said.

"Yes." Connor said.

I was rather stunned. Me and Connor had never actually given a title to our relationship, and now in front of all my family and friends he said we were boyfriend and girlfriend. I was unsure how I felt about this.

"Oh, well welcome Connor!" Sterben said.

"Where's fatty?" Dewar asked.

"Don't be rude, you little shit!" Mother yelled at Dewar.

"Ya, Dewar, don't be rude." I mocked then stuck out my tongue at him. (Childish, I know, but fun!)

Dewar gave me the finger.

Connor and I sat next to each other in the swinging couch mom had on the patio. I sat close to him and he put his arm around me. We sat around talking of this and that, when Kerri and Zeban showed up. When I first looked at Kerri my first thought was I was looking at a sausage that had been squeezed into a sleeve that was 10 times too small for it. Kerri was wearing a bright orange skirt that was so tight it was digging into her legs. She was wearing a pink tank top that ALMOST covered her breasts, but nothing else. My mother had to slap my brother in the back of the head from saying anything.

I didn't really know what to say. Zeban walked around the back of the couch to me.

"Dude I couldn't get her to change her clothes." He said.

"It's ok; I will see what I can do." I said.

"Kerri, sweetie. Why did you decide to where that?" I asked.

"Oh Aurroara, I was totally reading this new book. It's a series and I am on number 4. It is the Stephanie Plum series, by Janet Evanovich. I am trying to role model Lula. With the exception of the prostitute, thingy." She explained.

"Ummm, Kerri, that sounds great that you are trying something new, but I don't think orange and pink go together." I said trying to be nice.

"Of course they do otherwise they wouldn't have invented, Sherbert Ice cream!" She said.

"I'm sorry what. What does sherbert ice cream have to do with anything?" I asked.

"Think about there is Orange sherbert ice cream and there is pink sherbert ice cream. They are great on their own, but even better when you bring them together!" She explained to me.

I couldn't do anything but smile and nod.

"Well let's ask everyone else!" She said to me.

"Hey, what does everyone think of my new outfit?" She asked.

My brother opened his mouth, to say something when my mother interrupted him.

"This is Christy and John; they are neighbors from next door." My mother said at the people who had just come in the gate.

I sat there and thanked god for small favors. Kerri sat back down. Christy and John came in and sat down next to my mom. Christy unzipped her hoodie and a head popped out. It was what looked like a baby Chihuahua. This thing was tiny, about the size of a small cat. It looked out at everyone, and then jumped out of the hoodie and on to the ground. It came round and started sniffing everyone. It soon became very interested in Connor. Sniffing him, looking at him, and then sniffing him again. It was like it could see he was a human, but he smelled like an animal. Finally he couldn't figure it out and just climbed up in his lap and sat there. I smiled at Connor. The entire group sat there and talked about everything. I was really happy because they included Connor in their conversation. They liked him. It was nice. Dad started the grill and soon, put on the hot dogs, hamburgers, and brats and ribs. I helped mom bring out the potato salad, macaroni salad with cheese chunks and other stuff. We talked some more, then soon dinner was ready and there was less talking while everyone ate. After they ate they went and played horse shoes. Connor joined them. He teamed up with Sterben and everyone was in awww, when he got ringers and helped Sterben win the game. It was going great. I got up to go use the bathroom, and Syria followed me.

"Hey you I didn't see you come in." I said as I turned around and saw her there.

"I just got here. I am late because my lovely daughter had to get all prettified!" She explained.

"What have you been up to?" I asked.

"Nothing, you don't come see me anymore!" She said.

"I know I am just a horrible friend." I said.

"Yes you are, but I can look past your imperfections. That's what friends are for!" She said with a giggle.

"Nice!" I said smiling.

At that very moment I heard my mother scream "John take Christy home right now!"

Now normally my mother did not scream, but when she did you were better off not being on the receiving end of it. Me and Syria were still standing on the front porch, we hadn't made it to the bathroom. I looked over at were my mom was and saw Christy swinging that little Chihuahua over her head on a leash. I couldn't believe it. Me and Syria looked at each other, and then ran over to where my mother was. I saw Christy and John walking the other way towards their house next door. My mother was really pissed off.

"I cannot believe she would do that to that poor little puppy!" My mother yelled at no one in particular.

I walked over to Nama.

"What happened?" I asked.

"Well your mother said she wanted to get the place where the fireworks were going to be set off from ready. So Christy said she would help her. Everyone walked over there with them. I was saying how cute her dog was. Christy said do you want to see it do a trick. I said sure. She hooked the leash to it and started swinging it over her head. Your mother saw and told John to take her home. Ya she is totally pissed right now!" Nama explained.

Me and Nama walked back over to where everyone was playing horse shoes. I stood next to Connor and smiled as I saw him starring at me.

"What are you smiling about?" He asked.

"So you think I am your girlfriend do you? I don't remember you getting my permission for me to be your girlfriend!" I said with a sly smile.

He took my hand and smiled.

"Are you saying you don't want to be my girlfriend?" He asked.

"Are you kidding me? I'd love to be your girlfriend!" I said excitedly.

He laughed.

"I mean that sounds wonderful!" I said very lady like.

He smiled and kissed me.

The night had come and everything was dark. My brother and Sterben started setting off fireworks. Soon the sky was filled with beautiful light, in an array of colors. I stood there next to Connor. Then he looked at me and placed his hand on my cheek. He came closer to my face. I thought he was going to kiss me, but he whispered something in my ear.

"I love you!" He said.

I was stunned for a moment. I didn't know what to say. So I kissed him. A picture was taken from across the way. My mother took it. I looked at it when she brought over the digital camera. I could see a sparkler on the ground shooting up into the sky and right behind it was me and Connor kissing.

After the fireworks, we all went home. Me and Connor drove in silence holding hands. When I got home, he kissed me again. Then we walked to our own apartments. When I walked up to my door step, I saw a pink box tied up with a red ribbon. On it were the words "My Lovely, Aurroara!"

I unlocked the door and went in. I was closing the door when Kerri and Zeban walked in. Kerri sat down on the couch. Zeban looked at her.

"Ok I just have to say something. Kerri you look like a fat sausage they cook up for breakfast in a restaurant." He paused for a moment.

"Well a sausage that has gone bad anyways!" He finished his thought.

"I do not. I am sherbert ice cream, you moron!" She said.

"Ummm, sorry to disappoint you but ice cream isn't fattening looking, that's why people eat so much of it. It looks good. You look like a circus clown that went rogue and is out on a killing spree. Only you ate too many of the performers and now you can't kill anymore!" He said pointing at her.

"Well at least I don't look like a two legged monkey with an attitude!" Kerri said.

Zeban looked at her.

"You are a two legged monkey with an attitude!" He said calmly then walked to his room and closed his door.

I stood there in the living room still holding my unopened gift.

"Do you think I look like that?" She asked me.

"Now honestly she does look like a circus clown who ate too much" I thought, but

I would never tell her that.

"Kerri I think you look better in another color. This one just doesn't bring out your....your......your.....your eye color." I lied.

Kerri looked down. "Your right, this doesn't bring out the sparkle in my eyes. I will have to go shopping tomorrow." She said.

"Ummm Kerri you need a job to buy clothes to go shopping for." I said.

"Nope, David is paying!" She said and walked into the kitchen.

I walked into my room and closed my door. I sat on my bed and opened my gift. The ribbon slipped off and the box just opened itself. As the sides fell away a beautiful garnet rolled out onto the bed. My birthday being in January made my birth stone a garnet. How he knew that I didn't know.

"Come with me tonight to see the fireworks, from the sky!" A note inside the box said.

I held my breath. I wanted to go, I did. But every time I thought about calling him I kept hearing Connors voice in my head saying "I love you!" I didn't know what to do.

“Honestly Rio was only a friend and he knew about Connor, so it wasn't like I was cheating on Connor. I was just hanging out with a friend, right!" I said to myself. I called Rio and he said he would be at my house in a couple of minutes. I got all cute again, and put on some sensible riding clothes. Rio showed up just as I was walking out of my bed room door. He rang the door bell and Kerri answered with a sausage hanging out of her mouth. Rio started laughing.

"Is Aurroara here?" He asked.

"Ya, Aurroara!" Kerri yelled at the top of her lungs.

"Kerri, you don't have to yell I am right here!" I said annoyed.

I walked outside and got on Rio. We flew up into the clouds. I could see the stars dance in the sky. It was beautiful. Then the fireworks started. We were in the sky about 3 yards from them. It was wonderful being so close. Rio flew up and around them. We went in and out. Finally we landed on top of the mountain and sat there and watched. I could feel his eyes on me and I knew he wanted to kiss me. But he didn't touch me; it was like he read my mind and knew I could only give him friendship right now. After the fireworks were over, he took me home.

"You know, when he breaks your heart, I will be here for you!" He said and flew off.

'What in the world!!!!' I thought to myself.

Did Rio know something I didn't about Connor? How did Rio even know Connor? Why didn't I know? I had a lot of question and no answers. And worst of all I didn't know how to bring it up to Connor. So I went inside, flopped on my bed and let sleep envelope me into itself.

Chapter 16

I sat at the H desk wondering what Rio meant. His words went over and over in my head. "You know, when he breaks your heart. I will be here for you." Why would Connor break my heart? Did Rio know something about Connor I didn't?

"Excuse me! Excuse me!" The woman in front of me said.

"Yes, can I help you?" I asked rather annoyed.

"I am looking for a self help book!" She said.

"What kind of self help book?" I asked.

"It was the one I saw on the "Yesterday" show." she said.

"What was it called?" I asked.

"I don't know!" she said.

"What was the title?" I asked.

"I don't know!" she said.

"Is there anything you do know about this book?" I asked.

"Yes, it has a blue cover!" She said.

"Look we can't find books by color. We have to have title or author!" I explained.

"Well that's stupid!" She said.

"You know ma'am, your right. Why don't I show you every blue book we have here in our library and you can tell me if the book you're looking for is one of them?" I said sarcastically.

"Well you don't have to get snippy about it!" she said.

"Well honestly ma'am, you're being stupid!" I said.

"Next!" I said to the next person in line.

The next person walked up. I was busy watching the idiot lady walk out, that I didn't notice who it was.

"Connor!" I shouted a little louder then I meant.

"Hey gorgeous!" He said.

"What are you doing here?" I asked.

"Well I just talked to Kerri and she said she is having a dinner party with her new boyfriend and she thought it would be nice if me and you came together." He said.

"That sounds great!" I said.

"Ok, it is at 7pm tonight." He said.

"Ok, I will see you then!" I said, thinking that it was the most non-steering discussion we ever had. I watched him leave and didn't really know what to feel. Tonight, we were supposed to be a happy couple having dinner with friends, but tonight I would feel the most uncomfortable, I just knew it.

I called up Kerri.

"Did you invite Connor and me to your dinner party tonight?" I asked.

"Yes, I would like to have others there. So there will be good conversation." she said.

"Oh...." was all I could get out.

"Why, is there something wrong?" she asked.

"Wrong, no. Just a little annoyed with some people right now!" I hung up thinking, "I have to get a hold of Rio and talk to him now!"

My shift was short, so once I finished I got my stuff and drove home. When I got there, I immediately went into my room and called Rio. He wasn't home, and he didn't pick up his cell phone. I looked at the clock and it was only 2. I had a couple of hours to track down Rio, and if I didn't get a hold of him he was going to be sorry. I flopped down on my bed and closed my eyes. I was just planning to lay there and think, but the next thing I knew I was a sleep. In my dream I was being torn apart by Rio and Connor. Both of them had an arm and were pulling. Like it was a tug of war, and I was the rope. I started screaming and woke myself up. I looked at the clock. It was 5:45. I got up and walked in to the living room. Kerri was running around like a chicken with her head cut off, holding a chicken with its head cut off.

"What are you doing with the chicken?" I asked her.

"I am looking for the boiling pot!" She said impatiently.

"It's under the counter." I said and went back into my room. I had to get dressed for this dinner party of Kerri's. I was defiantly not looking forward to it. I put on my black pants and tub top that made me look like the hottest thing ever. Hey if I was going to get into a fight with Connor tonight, I wanted him to see exactly what he was going to miss. I put on some make up and some perfume. When I was done I looked divine. I looked at the clock; it was fifteen minutes to seven. I sat on my bed. I wanted to be the last to arrive. I wanted to walk into the room once everyone had arrived and have them see how gorgeous I really was. At 7:15, I finally walked out. I got the exact reception I wanted. Connor's mouth dropped open and I felt like a queen. I looked right next to Connor and there sat another male. I assumed it was David, Kerri's new beau. I walked over and introduced myself.

"Hello I am Aurroara." I said.

"Hi, I'm David." He said shaking my hand.

His grip on my hand was firm, a little to firm. It was the kind of hand shake that said 'I am in charge, not you.'

I squeezed back, putting a little werewolf-ess into it, and oddly enough I got an even harder squeeze back. The look on my face must have been one that said 'WHAT THE HELL!' because he released my hand and walked into the kitchen with Kerri. This left me worried.

I sat next to Connor.

"Do you know him, or know anything about him?" I asked.

But before Connor got a chance to answer Kerri came beaming out of the kitchen,

"Dinner!" She giggled out.

Both me and Connor got up and walked into the dining room. On the table was a marvelous feast. An entire roast chicken, rolls, mashed potatoes, gravy, stuffing, green beans. Everything.

"WOW Kerri, you went all out." I said.

"Thanks, I hope you like it." She said.

“Where’s Julie?” I asked.

“She said she couldn’t make it because she was helping her mother pick out patterns for her new furniture.” Kerri said.

We all sat down and filled our plates. We were just about to eat when David opened his mouth and said "So Kerri tells me you’re a werewolf." Everyone's forks stopped half way to their mouths. Kerri blushed and I felt myself turn a shade of red.

"What?" I asked, as if I hadn't heard the tremendous rude acquisition that had just come out of his mouth.

"Kerri told me you are a werewolf." He stated again.

I didn't know how to how to answer this. I was taken back, and absolutely nothing would come out of my mouth. I shoved a roll in it, and said "I waa tha fuuu swwwww t eeee"

All three of the guests starred at me. I just smiled and chewed my roll. After I was finished David looked into my eyes.

"You know you are not the only werewolf at this table." He said.

I had to use all my strength not to look over at Connor. I looked at him with a puzzling look on my face. Then, I understood what he meant. I guess the realization was on my face because he smiled.

"That's right I am one as well. And so is your little lover Connor!" He said with a sly smile.

I sat there and didn't really know what to say or think. I looked at Connor.

"Do you know David?" I asked.

"Aurroara, I have known David for a few years, yes." He said.

"Aurroara, I think you need to join us. We werewolves are the strongest and most powerful force on earth. We should be ruling this planet not hiding from, these measly humans. We have a group that is made up of nothing but werewolves. We are the better species. We are the smarter ones. We deserve to be in charge." He explained.

I sat there taking it all in. I looked over at Connor.

"Is this what you believe?" I asked him.

"Of course it is what he believes. That is why he is with you. To recruit you. Do you honestly think he just ran into you by chance?" He said laughing.

I was beginning to grow angry.

I looked at Connor.
"Is that true?" I asked.

"Sort of, yes I was sent to recruit you, but I fell in love with you. Please believe me when I tell you that my mission wasn't the only thing that kept bringing me back to you. I love you!" He said.

"Don't be ridiculous Connor. The mission is the important objective here." David said.

I had heard enough, I was about to explode and unfortunately I did. All over Kerri's new boyfriend. I jumped from my seat and transformed in mid air. I wrestled David to the ground. My anger pushing me to the point of insanity. David had transformed and was ready for me, or at least that was what he thought. When

I had leapt through the air, I had leapt with such force brought on by the anger that I completely took David down. I was on top of him bearing my teeth and I could see the surprise in his eyes. A look that said 'he had never been lunch before, just the hunter.' Connor came up from behind me and placed his human hand on my shoulder. I turned and looked into his eyes. I transformed back into my human self, and got off of David. I turned and walked into my room to dress myself. I could hear David and Connor talking from the other room.

"What the hell was that, Connor?" David shouted.

"I'm sorry, but she has a temper." Connor said.

"I can see that. What I want to know is why you didn't tell me about it. She completely defeated me. No one has ever been able to do that. She is strong, possibly even stronger than me. We need her." David said.

"David, are you alright?" I heard Kerri say, when she finally came out of shock.

"Yes, yes stop annoying me. I am trying to talk." He said.

"Excuse me! I am your girl friend." Kerri yelled at him.

"Look sweetie, the only reason I dated you was to get close to Aurroara. I am here, so you can go!" He said.

I walked to the door frame of my bedroom, and saw Kerri's eyes fill up with tears. She punched him in the face and kept hitting him, screaming "Bastard, you bastard!" David whirled around in one movement transforming at the same time. He was on top of Kerri in a flash of fur. I changed and reached down and lifted him off her and carried him to the door. I plopped him on the front porch and transformed back into my sexy human self.

"You listen to me, you butt munch. Kerri is a respectable lady and you will treat her like one, got it? And FYI you don't need to bother, cause I sooooo don't want to join a club for lonely bitches and their pets. So get up, get off my front porch and get the hell out of here!" I yelled.

David looked in at Connor. Connor walked to the door.

“You don’t have to leave, Connor. Just the ass hole!” I explained.

Connor gave me an I’m sorry look. A tear rolled down my face when I realized that Connor was choosing the werewolf alliance over me.

Chapter 17

I called in sick to work today. I couldn’t face the world. Not today. There was a knock at the door. I ignored it. I just wanted to lay here and be alone. Connor had chosen those idiot’s over me. The one who in the same night confessed he loved me. How on god’s green earth was that even possible. I thought about the time he left because he thought I was with another werewolf, but this. This was different. This wasn’t a misunderstanding. This was what it was, and this was him leaving me for them. No words, no good-byes. I laid there and looked at the darkness around me. There was another knock on the door, again I ignored it.

“Aurroara, are you there?” Kerri’s voice came through the door.

I was about to yell “Leave me the hell alone!” When I realized that Kerri was probably feeling just as lonely as I was. David had left her, just as Connor had left me. I got up and opened the door. I saw her on the other side. The tears she had cried had stained her face. I felt for her. I put my arm around her and led her into my room. She started crying again.

“It does get better.” I said.

“I hope so. I hate feeling like this. Why would he do this to me?” She asked me.

“Because he is a douche bag. That’s why. You heard him. He thinks he is god’s gift to….well everything! He doesn’t care about anyone, but himself.” I explained.

Kerri looked at me.

“Thanks for what you did last night. You didn’t have to.” She said.

“Yes, I did. You’re my best friend. And god knows I have to blame someone when

Zeban starts complaining about his chewed up shoes." I laughed.

Kerri laughed as well.

"I'm sorry about Connor. I know how much he means to you." Kerri said.

"Thanks. I really thought Connor cared for me, but it turns out he is just another ass-hole." I said angrily.

"What about Rio?" Kerri asked.
I looked at her and smiled. I hadn't thought about Rio in a while. I sat in thought for a minute.
"Wait a minute. Rio new this was going to happen. He told me 'You know, when he breaks your heart. I will be here for you.' Rio somehow knew Connor was going to do this. How? I don't know. But I am going to find out." I said.

I grabbed my phone and called Rio's cell phone. I got his message machine.

"Rio, ummm ya we need to talk. NOW! How did you know Connor was going to ditch me? And how did you know that he was going to break my heart? Call me. Oh this is Aurroara." I said.

I looked at Kerri.

"Let's go get some ice cream." I said.

She nodded. I could see another tear rolling down her check.

The next day I felt better. Not by much, but enough to go back to work. I walked in and noticed that the alarm had started going off. Usually someone was there ahead of me and shut it off. I noticed five cars in the parking lot. So I know I wasn't the only one there. I punched in my code and shut off the alarm. I walked to the front desk and noticed that it was rather quite for a Friday morning, unusually quite. I turned on the security monitor above my head; I would be able to find anyone in the library with it. I looked at each of the cameras and noticed something rather odd going on in the community room. I zoomed in on that particular camera. What I saw surprised me. I saw all the employees sitting on the floor and about 20 men with guns. I grabbed the cordless phone and called 911. When I got the operator I told her who I was and what I saw. She said she was sending the police and I should stay on the line. I heard a gunshot and accidently hit the off button. I ran back to the cameras and looked. I saw Hellzone on the floor with blood coming out of his arm. I knew I couldn't just stand there. I walked to the community room. The men saw me and stared. One grabbed me by the arm and started to drag me to the others. I snatched my arm from him and he slapped me hard across the face. Exactly what I expected him to do. My anger rose up and I transformed. I started beating the crap out of the men with the guns. Soon Catherine started kicking some of the other men with her hind legs. Then even Peter our Poltergeist got in on the action. He stood in front of one of the men and when the other guy was about to hit him, he went invisible and the guy hit his own man. Then Peter laughed and floated away. Even Jillian the little fairy would grab the men by the nose hairs and pull. By the time we were done with them, the cops showed up and they were begging to be taken away. I had calmed down and changed back to a human and before I had a chance to hide, everyone starred at me and my naked-ness. One of the cops draped his coat around my shoulders and I walked to the bathroom. I had kept clothes in my locker, just in case and the cop got me my clothes and brought them to me. After I finished dressing, I walked out in time to see Hellzone being carted away on a stretcher.

"Wait, Wait." I yelled at the paramedics.

They stopped and looked at me.

"Is he going to be alright?" I asked.

"Yes, it is just a flesh wound. We have to take him to the hospital, your employer wants us to. It is just procedure." He said.

I smiled.

"I will see you later, Hellzone." I said and waved good-bye.

I went back inside and found the rest of them. Jillian decided to close the library so the police can look in the community room without any people getting in their way. I was on my way to my car when I heard Jillian calling me.

"Aurroara, wait a minute." She said.

I stopped and turned to face her.

“I want to thank you for everything you did. You saved every one’s life here today.” She said.

“I didn’t do anything, someone else wouldn’t have done.” I said.

“Yes, but you saw the situation, analyzed it and took control of it. You will be a great leader. You already are.” She said with a smile.

“Thank you.” I said smiling.

She turned flittered to her car (she had a driver because she was too small to reach the petals) and I turned and walked to mine. It wasn’t often I got complimented by Jillian. I got to my car and Rio was sitting next to it.

“Hey.” I said.

“Hey.” He said.

“So, tell me how you know that Connor was going to break my heart.” I said.

“David tried to recruit me for his stupid cause last month. I saw him looking at a list of names of people they wanted to recruit. Your name was on it. When I delivered the flowers, I saw your name on the card and put 2 and 2 together.” He explained.

“So why didn’t you just tell me about his stupid cause?” I asked.

“Would you have believed me? A stranger you just met telling you that the guy you love is just trying to recruit you for his group.” He asked.

“No, probably not.” I said.

I didn’t know what to say after that. So I just stood there.

“Rio, I don’t know what to do. I am so angry with Connor right now!” I started to say.

“Don’t say anything. Just listen. I really like you. You make me smile every time I think about you. I love it when you smile and laugh. You are the best thing I could ever ask for. Please, all I ask is that you don't exclude me. I understand Connor has traits I don't have, but I can love you the same way he does. Just think about it." He said then took off into the air.

As I watched him fly off I heard my phone go off. I looked at who was calling, it said "Connor".

I pressed the 'send' button.

"Hello." I said.

"Hi, can we talk?" He asked.

"Yes, were do you want to meet?" I asked.

"How about that Mexican restaurant behind Wally-world?" He asked.

"Ok I will meet you there in half an hour." I said.

I drove home and put on something cute. Then drove out to 'Beans R Us'. The Mexican Restaurant behind wally-world. When I got there, I parked and got out of my car. As I did I smelled the air. There was a scent I knew, but couldn't place it. It was soft like it was masked by something else. I walked inside. I saw Connor by the table next to the window. I slid into the booth.

"Look I am sorry about everything, you have no idea how sorry I am." He said.

"Then why did you do it?" I asked angrily.

"Because it is my job to get new recruits and David really wanted you, and after what happened the other night I know why. You have strength never seen by other werewolves, and god knows what else." He said.

"That's not true. Your strong, remember when we first met you completely took me down!" I said.

"Yes, I remember; but you seem to get……. I don't know what to call it. Ubber strength, especially when you get mad. You took down David like he was a twig, and he is the strongest one of us." He said.

“Connor, do you really believe that stupid shit David is spouting?” I asked.

“Honestly at first I did, now I don’t.” He said.

“Then why don’t you leave?” I asked.

“It’s not that easy. Once you’re a member you’re a member for life.” He said.

“That’s right, sweetie. Once you become a member, you are part of the family.” David said.

I turned and saw him. He was standing next to me with about 10 of his friends. He reached over and tried to sit down next to me, I growled. He got up and sat next to Connor.

“I think your friends need to leave before I get pissed off.” I said to David.

One of them, a black haired young man. I would assume was no older then about 25 stepped closer to me. I stood up.

“Gentlemen, wait outside.” David said.

They all traipsed out the door. I sat back down.

“What do you want David?” I asked.

“Aurroara, you have magnificent powers that go with being a werewolf. None of us posses. We need you to be part of us.” He said.

“No. How did you find out about my abilities anyway? You can’t say Connor, because not even I knew of my super abilities of strength when I get mad until I took them out on you.” I said sternly.

“Well at first Connor here was obsessed with you. Watching you from his living room and wanting to meet you. Then when he saw you turn and take down that man who tried to rape you, I thought it would be a good idea for another recruit. Werewolves are stronger in numbers. I told Connor we had to have you. I want as many werewolves in my command as I can. I want them all! Then when you showed your wonderful abilities at the dinner the other day, it was just icing on the cake. When Connor told you he loved you, he does. But now he is only aloud to be with you if I say so, and that permission is only given to those in our group. So I am going to ask you again would you like to join us?" He asked.

"No!" I said.

"I didn't want to have to do this, but you give me no chose." David said.

I saw him pull out a knife from his pocket and stick it against Connors side.

"We werewolves are fast, but I will plunge this into Connors side before he has a chance to move. Now, I am asking nicely. Join us." David said.

At that point my heart skipped a beat and I felt myself leave my body. I saw myself grab the knife from David's hand and then I returned to myself with it. I looked down into my hand and there was the knife.

"Well, do you want me to stab your love with a knife?" David said.

"Oh you mean this knife." I said showing him the knife and smiling.

David looked into his hand. The knife he was holding was gone.

"Outer body transportation!" Connor said.

"I thought Connor was the love of my life, but it turns out he'd rather be your lap dog, then my lover. I don't want any part of your little family." I said.

I looked at Connor, "Any part." Then I got up and walked out.

Chapter 18

As I walked to my car I saw the group of David's flunky's watch me. I opened my purse and reached for my keys. I took them out and was about to unlock my car door when I heard.

"Get her! Don't let her get away!" Coming from David's mouth. He was standing in the doorway of the restaurant.

The flunky's looked at David then at me. Then started running for me. I was about to change when Rio came out of the sky. He landed next to me.

"Need some help?" He asked.

"How did you know I was here?" I asked.

"Over heard your conversation when you were on the phone at the library. He said.

"Oh." I said.

Then the pack of creepy k-9 crawlers hit us. Rio was holding his own. Holding back five of them. I was fighting the other five. I saw David standing at the door to the restaurant and I wanted to tear him to pieces. I punched a brown one in the nose hitting him so hard he was pushed back into a car and knocked out. A black one I bit in the leg so hard I felt his bones crush beneath my teeth. The light blondish one I just picked up and threw, the other two Rio grabbed. As he dealt with them I ran towards David. I saw Connor look at David then at me. Then I saw him transform and lunge at me. As he did I rolled under him and was on top of David ready to rip his throat out. Then Connor ran up behind me and clawed my back. The pain was infuriating. I screamed. Well I screamed on the inside, but it only came out as a high pitched howl. I fell to the ground. I laid there for a few seconds and heard hoofs. They were beating down on the pavement. I looked up just in time to see Connor jump up and dig his claws into Rio's neck. Connor started on the back left side and swung around to the right all the while his claws were in bedded in Rio. I saw blood coming out of Rio's back. Then I saw him go down.

I got up off the ground. I stood there and saw David's little pack walk up behind Connor. I could feel my blood boil, my skin heat and my sense were leaving. I was beyond 'PISSED OFF!'

I walked slowly over to Connor. He looked at me. I grabbed him by the throat picked him up off the ground with my left arm, and then threw him on to the black top. I knelt there for a moment. I saw the pack back away, and then run off. I turned around and David was gone. I knelt down to Connor's ear.

"Get out of here, NOW!" I said.

I then stood up and ran over to Rio.

Chapter 19

I knelt down next to Rio. I didn't know what to do. He was only half human. What hospital would I call? I decided to get my cell phone out of my pocket and calling 911, it was better than nothing. The only problem was I had no pockets, because I had no clothes on. I felt a hand on my shoulder. I looked up and saw a man. He covered my shoulders with his jacket.

"Hello, Aurroara. I am Derek." He said.

"How do you know my name?" I asked.

"Do you really think the werewolves are the only ones watching someone like you?" He asked.

I honestly never really thought about it.

"We know what David is trying to do, so we watch everything he does and everyone he tries to recruit." Derek said.

"We saw what happened at your friends dinner party. You have some special gifts that can help a lot of people." He said.

"Can my gifts help Rio?" I asked him.

He looked at me with an expression of unknown. As if he didn't know if he should or shouldn't help me.

"No you can't, but I can. There is a condition that comes with it though. " He said.

"When it comes time I will ask you for a favor." He said.

"I am not sleeping with you!" I blurted out.

"What...... NO! You know it's true ALL you werewolves have dirty minds." HE said.

"Ya, we are earth lovers. We love to play in the mud. Duhhh!" I said.

He raised his left eyebrow at me as if to say 'Whatever!'

"What are you going to do?" I asked.

"First of all, do you accept the terms?" He asked.

"Yes, yes. At some point you will ask me for a non-sexual favor. Fine. I will oblige your request to the best of my abilities. Now help him!" I said.

"Aurroara, I am going to tell you right now this isn't easy. Ok." He said.

I didn't really know what he meant by that. But I said "Ok." Anyway.

Derek bent over Rio, I then saw him bear four fangs. Derek was a vampire. I didn't want to watch, but I couldn't look away. Derek bit down into Rio's skin and started sucking. After about five minutes he stopped. He lifted himself off Rio and looked at me. Rio lay lifeless.

"He's not moving!" I said.

"Give it a few minutes. It takes a few minutes for the vampire venom I pumped into him to take effect." He said.

Rio's body started to shake. I stood up and moved back.

“Is that supposed to happen?” I asked.

“Yes, the body is trying to figure out what its new shape will be.” He said.

“New Shape! What the hell does that mean?” I screamed

“Vampire blood is pure. No matter who bites you it all comes from one main source. His name is Dra. Since his blood is pure so is ours. When I bit him he got that pure blood. His body is now trying to figure out whether my blood is stronger or his. If his is he will remain a Pegaman, and it will just heal him. If it is mine he will transform back into a man and become a vampire.” He explained.

I looked at him, my eyes as big as cannon balls.

“Why didn’t you tell me this before?” I asked.

“I did. I told you it wasn’t going to be easy.” He said.

“That’s not explaining to me that my future boyfriend might be a vampire.” I shouted.

He looked at me. I was about to yell some more when I looked over at Rio. He stopped shaking and his body had taken it’s form.

Chapter 20

"I have one hell of a headache." Rio said.

He was still lying on the ground, with me and Derek standing over him.

"Rio, I want you to listen to me. There is something I need to tell you." I said.

I then sat beside him and explained everything that happened with the fight with the werewolves and with Derek. I then explained about the little explanation Derek conveniently did not mention to me about the possibility of Rio's body transforming.

"So what happened? Which one did the blood choose?" Rio asked. He looked down at the lower half of his body. He was human.

"OH MY........" He started, then stopped.

"You're a vampire." Derek said as if congratulating him.

Rio tried standing. I helped him. He spent his entire life on four legs now with only two it was hard to find balance.

Rio looked at his body. Touching every part of it. His body as a Pegaman was white. A silky shiny white. His body as a human was a beautiful caramel color. His hair was black and his eyes were the color of dark chocolate with a beautiful blue ring around the brown. I looked away when he opened his pants to look there.

"I'm sorry Rio. It was the only way I could save your life." I said.

"I understand. It will take some getting used to. I think the biggest thing is not being able to fly anymore." He said.

"What are you talking about. We fly." Derek said floating five feet off the ground.

I saw Rio's eye light up. He was still using me as a crutch, but he was able to lift himself off the ground about an inch. He came back down and we walked to my car. Rio sat in the back seat while I put on a pair of pants and a shirt from my trunk. Then Derek came walking over to us.

"Aurroara about that favor." He said.

"Ya." I said.

"There is a war brewing. David and his pack are getting out of control. They have to be taken out! Can we count you as one of us, to fight against David?" He asked.

I smiled.
"Yes, nothing would give me more pleasure then to kick David's ass!" I said.

"Very well. We will contact you when the time comes." He said, then flew off.

I got into the driver's seat and Rio got out of the back and into the passenger seat. He looked over at me.

"You know when I was laying on the ground I remember hearing you say 'That is not explaining to me that my future boyfriend might be a vampire." He said with a smile.

"You heard that huh." I said.

"Ya, but I think we should change that future boyfriend to present boyfriend. What do you think?" He said as he reached over and slowly kissed me.

I looked at him, smiled and said "I love that idea."

Then I kissed him.

Chapter 21

There are very few things I really know about myself.

One is I am in love with a vampire. Two I am an ubber hot Librarian/werewolf-ess with a nice ass, (or at least that's what Rio keeps telling me.) Three there was a war coming. A war I am a part of. David I could take down he was the man I wanted to hunt down the most. Connor.....Connor was different. He was the man that infiltrated all my defenses and stole my heart, then shredded it in front of my face.

Did I hate him? No.
Did I love him? No.
Did I still have feelings for him? Yes.

I didn't want him back, but I knew deep within myself I could never kill him. We had once loved each other and that memory would always be in my head, and that scared me. How can I fight a man I could not kill?

Made in the USA
Coppell, TX
01 December 2021